MURDER IN ZAIRE VALLEY

THEASTARR VALERIE

A Nhyira Files Mystery

Empress Royále
Publishing

Murder In Zaire Valley
A Nhyira Files Mystery

Copyright © 2019 Theastarr Valerie

ISBN: 9781733829304

Editors: Theastarr Valerie, Akilah Valerie – Empress Royále Publishing
        Email: empressroyalepublishing@gmail.com

Cover Design: Empress Royále Publishing

Cover Photo: "Foggy Forest" from StockSnap (Pixabay.com)
        "Cosmetics" from OpenClipart-Vectors (Pixabay.com)
        "Magnifying Glass" from *Bru-nO* (Pixabay.com)

Empress Royále Publishing

"Everything tells a story; let us help you tell your story to the world."

Email: empressroyalepublishing@gmail.com

DEDICATION

To all the men and women who have devoted their lives to solving mysteries.

To all the Parents, Educators, Members of the Judiciary System, Medical Professionals, Mystery Lovers, Problem Solvers, Researchers, Authors...

This book is for you.

Thank you for all your hard work.

Proverbs 25:2 (KJV)

"*It is the glory of God to conceal a thing: but the honour of kings is to search out a matter.*"

To God, the greatest mystery writer from eternity to eternity, thank You.

CHAPTER 1

Zaire Valley Realty

AUCTION

This Friday at 2:00PM
Veisiejai House
Njapa, Zaire Valley

Please call to register for the auction.
Agent: D. Sellers
Phone Number: *88-01-20-4420

1 Murder In Zaire Valley

Flipping through the radio stations, Nhyira Enosis puts her **Epitome X Series** 1 into sports mode, excited at the chance to test drive her new car. She was minutes away from her potential dream house: a 40-year-old mansion in *Njapa, Zaire Valley*, Celgagoas.

A native of *Grape Fjord*, Mt. Thafivin, she was known as **The** Spelling Bee Champ. Nhyira had a natural ability to unscramble any word from the dictionary. And no one could deny her fascination for unsolved mysteries. When she read the ad for the abandoned house up for auction, she knew that it had to be hers.

With her inheritance in her purse she mashed the gas pedal. If she missed the auction, someone else would bid on the house. That was a setback she couldn't afford.

Mr. Sellers had the perfect house for Nhyira. As the top Real Estate Agent in *Zaire Valley*, he knew how to match the perfect house with its perfect owner. This particular house however, remained unsold for decades. No one in the country was interested in procuring a house formerly owned by a man whose wife murdered him in cold blood.

The mystery of the old **Veisiejai House** remained since 1958. It was a part of *Njapa's* history that none of its residents dared to speak about. Only a handful of citizens knew what *really* happened on that fateful night.

Placing an ad in the newspaper for an auction, Mr. Sellers hoped that someone outside of Celgagoas would be willing to purchase the house, despite its obscure history.

Ten minutes later, Nhyira turns off her car.

This is it. I really hope I get this house.

"I'm here," Nhyira says, walking up to her agent. "Am I too late? Is the auction over?"

"You're on time," Mr. Sellers replies, extending his hand.

Nhyira shakes the man's hand politely, looking around the mansion grounds. "Where is everyone?"

"You're the only person who responded to the ad."

She stares in awe at the mansion. "Why would anyone pass up this opportunity?"

The duo walk towards the entrance.

"Welcome to the **Veisiejai House**," he announces.

"Since I'm the only one here, does that mean I got the house?"

"Are you sure it's to your liking?"

Nhyira nods.

"Come inside, I'll give you a tour," Mr. Sellers motions.

"The mansion has 50 rooms. 4 master suites, 10 guest bedrooms, 2 kitchens: one in the main house and the other out back in the workers' quarters, a library…" Mr. Sellers explains to a beaming Nhyira.

Nhyira observes the majestic stairwell of the mansion, thinking about her childhood home. After her parents died, she inherited a large sum of money: $100,000 to be exact. But she had to wait until her 21st birthday to receive it.

Being placed in the foster system at the age of 14, Nhyira was determined to overcome the statistics of unsuccessful orphans. Soon after her mother and father passed, she delved into books at the orphanage; her favorite book being the dictionary. It was an abnormal connection, but in the end it proved to be beneficial.

The National *Grape Fjord* Spelling Bee was a yearly event. Nhyira won 5 consecutive years and retired at 20. Her community nicknamed her **The Grape Fjord Unscrambler,** a name she cherished.

She received her PhD at 21 - a feat not many her age accomplished - majoring in Linguistics and History. Now it was time for the next step: her own home.

"What do you think?" Mr. Sellers asks, stopping her flashback.

"I love it," Nhyira squeals.

Mr. Sellers lifts his brows in astonishment, "Really?"

"Isn't this what you wanted, someone to buy the house?"

"You have no idea how happy you've made me. The commission that I'm going to get from selling this mansion is going to put me on the map. Thank you Ms. Enosis."

"Are you crying?" she chortles.

"Just a little dust," he says, wiping his obvious tears.

Nhyira hoped that she could convince the agent to give her a better deal. "Do you think that you can lower the asking price? I can't use all of my savings to purchase the mansion."

"It's fully furnished," the agent scoffs. "This house is worth more than the asking price."

Not backing down from her stance, Nhyira continues, "I may decide to renovate and I need money."

Mr. Sellers exhales, "I'll see what I can do."

"Please try," Nhyira pleads. "I really want this house."

An hour later Nhyira's phone rings.

"It's yours," Mr. Sellers exclaims over the phone.

"I got it?"

"I'm happy to finally have it off the market. You can have the house for $55,000. I'll bring the keys and paperwork later."

"Perfect. This calls for a celebration." Nhyira clicks off her phone, scanning the neighborhood for an eatery.

CHAPTER 2

The bell over the door pings as Nhyira enters a diner.

Mayleigh's Diner was the busiest spot in town. Known for her famous *Plumberry Pancakes*, Mayleigh smiled every time a new customer arrived.

"Night. What's your name honey?" a woman with brown highlights greets.

"Nhyira."

"Sounds exotic. I'm Mayleigh, the owner. Where're you from?"

"Mt. Thafivin."

"Never been. Hungry?"

"What do you have that tastes good?" Nhyira replies, pretending to scan the menu.

Mayleigh stands akimbo. "Why everything on my menu's delicious. But, round these parts we're known for our *Plumberry Pancakes*."

"I don't think I've ever eaten *Plumberry Pancakes*."

"Of course not. It's only sold here in *Njapa*," Mayleigh giggles.

"Okay. I'll try it."

"Do you want to add a drink to your order?"

Nhyira glances at the menu before stating, "*Emerald Smoothie.*"

"Coming right up." Mayleigh heads to the kitchen to give the chef Nhyira's order.

"Night Mayleigh. I'll have the usual," a man in uniform announces upon arrival.

"I'll be right with you," Mayleigh responds.

The man turns and sees Nhyira at the other end of the counter. His eyes extend, "Wow, good night beautiful."

"Thanks Mayleigh. You were right. Those pancakes are delicious. I'll be back." Nhyira makes her way to the exit.

Not used to being ignored the man stops Nhyira in her tracks. "Don't you have any manners?"

"Oh I'm sorry. I didn't notice you. I thought you were speaking to Mayleigh."

"Nhyira's new in town," Mayleigh announces.

"Clearly not too friendly," he mumbles.

"Again, I'm sorry," Nhyira apologizes.

"Akio Qvareli," the man declares, extending his hand.

Nhyira opts out of the handshake, staring at the door she wanted to exit. "What?"

"My name in case you were wondering," Akio adds.

"Actually I wasn't. Thanks again Mayleigh. See you later," she says, walking out of the diner.

Moments later, Mayleigh playfully hits Akio with a dish towel. "That's not how you talk to a lady."

"She's obviously uncouth; didn't even acknowledge my presence."

"Hate to burst your bubble Akio, but not every girl is swayed by your charm."

Akio looks at the door and smirks. "What charm?"

"Watch it," Mayleigh warns. "Nhyira doesn't know about your reputation as a heartbreaker."

"That was the past."

"I gotta get back to work. Leave her alone, I'm warning you. She seems like a nice girl," Mayleigh replies.

Back at the mansion, Nhyira closes the door behind Mr. Sellers. She exhales in relief. The house was officially hers.

Nhyira plops down on the couch. From the distance she notices what looked like a scratch on the living room table.

I hope I don't have to buy new furniture just yet.

Kneeling down, she places her hand on the indentation.

"That's odd. It looks like a letter."

T

Shrugging her shoulders, Nhyira makes her way upstairs. One little scratch wasn't going to ruin her purchase.

Inside her bedroom Nhyira yawns, allowing the warmth of the house to consume her. Making her way to the bathroom she drops her bath caddy on the floor.

There was another carving on the floorboard next to her bed. This couldn't be a coincidence. It was another letter.

T

Two T's? Could this be a clue to a mystery?

Turning on the showerhead, Nhyira laughs. She was undoubtedly fatigued.

CHAPTER 3

Later that night, Nhyira crosses the street with her homemade *Miomei Pasta* in hand. She was eager to meet her neighbor, as there were no other houses nearby.

Mr. Sellers informed her that the two houses were marked as historical relics and couldn't be demolished when the park was built.

Standing in front of the house, Nhyira raps on the door, noting the exquisite brass knocker. Her neighbor peers out. Immediately, Nhyira guesses the woman to be about 65.

"May I help you?"

"Hello. My name is Nhyira Enosis; I am your new neighbor. I made you some *Miomei Pasta*."

The old woman scrunches up her nose. "Keep your food. What do you want?"

"What's your name?"

"Ms. Higüey. What do you want?"

"I thought we should get to know one another since we're the only two living in this area."

With matted hair and a tattered robe, the woman closes the door behind her. Nhyira felt sorry for her.

"If I were you, I'd pack up my possessions and high tail it out of that house. The previous owner's deceased," Ms. Higüey mumbles.

"I got all the historical details from my agent. That's what fascinated me in the first place. Besides, it was the lowest price I got for a house, couldn't pass it up," Nhyira shrugs.

"The last stranger who lived in that house killed her husband. I don't trust you foreigners."

"I was born in Starr Islands, hardly a foreigner."

"You're stubborn. Suit yourself. Just stay off my property. I've been fine living alone for all these years. Goodbye," she shouts, slamming the door.

Giving the door a once over, Nhyira shrugs and skips across the street with her untouched pasta dish. A smirk spreads across her face. The journey ahead was bound to be an exciting one.

I have to get that young lady out of that mansion by any means necessary... Ms. Higüey thinks as she closes her window shutters.

CHAPTER 4

The following morning, Nhyira opens the town's library door, eager to obtain information about the **Veisiejai House** mystery.

"Good morning," Nhyira greets the librarian.

"How may I help you miss?"

"Where can I find information about the town's history?"

The librarian frowns at Nhyira, "We're not into history. But, there are a few articles in the back."

"I'll take whatever I can get. I love history."

"Right this way," the gray haired librarian states, leading Nhyira to the archives.

"You can look through these documents as long as you remain silent," the librarian warns.

Nhyira beams at the dusty room. "I will."

"I'm out front if you need any assistance. You can't take anything out from the archives."

"Thanks," Nhyira nods with understanding.

Nhyira skims through a few files and yawns.

There's nothing of substance in here.

Just then she spots a catchy article title from 1958. Picking up the article, she begins to read...

Njapa Woman Arrested For Murder

February 28, 1958

It's a sad day in *Njapa*, Zaire Valley as residents mourn the loss of their beloved **Mr. Popular**.

21 year old Poet Veisiejai has been arrested in the murder of her husband, 25 year old *Njapa* Construction Magnate, Kavos Veisiejai, dubbed **Mr. Popular** by residents of Zaire Valley.

Poet was found guilty of first degree murder of Kavos Veisiejai on February 27th, according to a Zaire Valley District Attorney's statement.

Police responded to an anonymous call around 8PM stating that they'd seen a strange person walk through the side of the **Veisiejai House** dressed in all black. Poet was the only person home, the caller stated.

In an initial interview with officers, Mrs. Veisiejai indicated that she was a heavy sleeper and did not hear what happened at the time of the alleged attack.

She had no blood on her hands when the officer arrived and stated she had not seen her husband for the day.

Several neighbors told police that Poet was known as a flirt and was accused of having an affair with the town's mayor.

They also said that Mrs. Veisiejai kept to herself.

The Medical Examiner ruled the death a homicide. No further details are being released to the public at this point.

Mrs. Veisiejai has been sentenced to life in prison for this heinous act committed against the town's beloved citizen.

The contents of the article piqued Nhyira's interest and she runs to the front desk.

Nhyira clears her throat.

The librarian looks up from her computer. "Is everything alright?"

"Do you have any other files on the Veisiejai's?"

The librarian stares at Nhyira in confusion.

"I read the article about the murder at the **Veisiejai House**."

"Young lady, it's been forty years. There's no information. What you see is all we have."

"What can you tell me about Mr. Veisiejai?"

"Never met the man, but he was one of the founding fathers of *Njapa*. Before he moved here, there were a few houses, but mostly miles of open fields. He built many of the structures you see here in town, including this library."

"Were you born in *Njapa*?" Nhyira inquires.

"I moved here about 5 years after Mr. Veisiejai's death," the librarian states. "I was 16 at the time. I was born in Trinidad, an island located in the West Indies."

"Where'd he come from?"

"I'm not privy to that information."

Nhyira's mind begins to race with questions, "No birth records?"

"Back in those days they didn't keep birth records here. Everyone knew one another and that was all that mattered."

"Starr Islands has always been advanced, there has to be records somewhere," Nhyira continues.

"Look child, I told you what I know," the librarian responds, agitated.

"I didn't get your name."

"Mrs. Denoble."

"My name's Nhyira. Thanks for all your help."

"Feel free to visit anytime."

"I will," Nhyira calls out, exiting the library.

A smirk forms on Nhyira's face as she strolls to her car.

A mystery? Sounds like my cup of tea. I have to find out more about Mr. Veisiejai. How could he live in a town where no one knows his origins? Or is it that they do know, but don't want to share? Njapa, you are a peculiar little town.

CHAPTER 5

The crisp night air pierced through Nhyira's gray and lilac hoodie. She slides her hands in the pockets to begin her run through the park.

Living in a secluded area of town gave her freedom to roam. Besides Ms. Higüey, there was no one to disturb her privacy. The local park surrounding her house went on for miles.

It'd been two weeks since she moved into her new home and she finally decorated the main part of the house to her standards.

Being 22 didn't exempt her from health issues, so she vowed to remain physically active.

Nhyira stopped at the park's edge. From there she could see the main shops in town: **Mayleigh's Diner**, a Vet clinic, boutique, and the grocery. She didn't mingle much with the residents and her neighbor hadn't reached out to her.

She decided to start reading the books found in the mansion's library. Mr. Veisiejai's collection was immense.

One of the books that caught her attention was *Vast Accusations* by *G.M. Zambesi; a* book written in the 1820s about unsolved mysteries from around the world. Who wouldn't want to curl up with a crime anthology?

According to Mr. Sellers, the previous owner's collection amounted to 1 Million original books, worth a fortune. Nhyira intended on reading them all.

"My night just got better," a man's voice trails in the distance.

Startled, Nhyira turns and stands face to face with the man from the diner. "What are you doing here?" she asks, uninterested.

"This is a public park. I come here to run sometimes."

"Remind me of your name again."

"You forgot?" the man replies, slightly insulted.

"Yes," Nhyira shrugs.

"Akio Qvareli," he grins.

"Ok cool."

"I never got your full name."

"Nhyira Enosis."

"Pretty."

"Thanks. Goodnight. I was just heading home."

"Can I run with you?" he offers.

"That's not necessary."

"Well," Akio counters, "I'll run to the other side of the park, and if it happens to be where you live, then…"

Ignoring her stance, Akio begins to run towards Nhyira's mansion.

"So this is the famous **Veisiejai House**," Akio observes, minutes later.

"You've never been here?"

"Not this close."

"Can I go inside now?"

"Wait," Akio sticks out his hands for emphasis.

"Yes?"

"Are you coming to the festival tomorrow night?"

"Festival?"

"*Njapa's* **Chocolate Festival**. We have it every year. It's our 26th year."

"Oh."

"You should come. Everyone brings a chocolate related dish to the festival and we share it. There are games, rides, contests, music and dancing. You'd love it. We even get people from other States coming."

"I'll think about it," Nhyira mumbles.

"I hope you come. I'll save a dance for you," he winks.

CHAPTER 6

Raising her head from the magazine Ms. Higüey looks petulantly at her neighbor's house. The sight made her cringe; another example of a foreigner coming to take over.

The young man waves to her and she pretends not to see him.

"Good night Ms. Higüey. How are you?"

"Why are you on my property?"

"I'm not," Nhyira states, pointing at the sidewalk.

"Why was he waving at me?"

"It's called being polite."

"What was he doing here?"

"Escorting me home."

"Hmph!" Ms. Higüey retorts, wrinkling her nose.

"What's your problem?" Nhyira scoffs.

"I don't trust outsiders."

"I'm your neighbor," Nhyira answers. "We should get to know one another."

"I'll pass."

"I won't force you to communicate, but I'll be around for the long haul. You cannot scare me or change my mind about buying the house."

"No respect for your elders," Ms. Higüey scolds.

"I haven't disrespected you. You older folks want young people to respect you, but don't lead by example. How does that make any sense?"

"You have some mouth on you, little girl."

"Have a good night Ms. Higüey." Nhyira turns and heads home, leaving the old woman stunned.

CHAPTER 7

The midday sun beamed through the kitchen window as Nhyira thought about the festival.

"What should I make for the festival? Chocolate to be exact. Who doesn't love chocolate? Oh I know, my *Chocolate Macadamia Cloud Torte*."

Nhyira begins to hum one of her favorite tunes, *Pretty Memories* by Starr Islands' top band, *The Miseno Brothers*.

The song brought her back to happier times with her parents. They'd always belt out the lyrics on top of their lungs when the bridge of the song came on.

"... I'll always have those prettyyyy memorieeeessss."

She smiled as she hummed the remaining verses.

Chocolate Macadamia Cloud Torte had been a family favorite. She'd learned to cook and bake from her mother, the baker extraordinaire of Mt. Thafivin. People came from miles just to buy her desserts.

Taking out the dishes from the cupboard, she places them in the sink. The house came fully furnished, but she didn't know how long the items had been in the cupboards. Cleanliness was imperative, so Nhyira decided to wash all of the dishes in the main kitchen. She'd tackle the second kitchen another time.

Drying the dishes, she places them in the cupboard one by one. Suddenly, her hand brushes against a gash on the left cupboard door. It was minute, but legible; another letter.

This time it was an E.

Dropping the dish towel on the counter, she runs upstairs to get her notebook to write down the latest letter.

She scribbles down the three letters she'd found. Next to each letter she writes the location she discovered them.

T T E

"What do these letters spell? TTE? That's not a word. ETT? Nah. Tet? No that can't be right. Hmmmm. What if there are other letters? Mr. Veisiejai what do these letters mean?"

She taps the pencil eraser on her lips, trying to think.

With no lightbulb going off in her head, she places the notebook on the counter and continues her baking. However, she couldn't shake the feeling that the previous owner left clues to something.

These aren't normal indentations. They aren't markings of a carpenter. The letters seem deliberately placed and strategically spaced out.

"What are you trying to tell me Mr. V?"

CHAPTER 8

The night sky filled the atmosphere with a serene ambiance.

Nhyira makes her way to the beach where the town held the festival. Out in the distance, she notices a house located at the other end of the coast.

"It's good to see you Nhyira. Welcome to **Njapa Chocolate Festival**. What did you bake?"

"*Chocolate Macadamia Cloud Torte,*" Nhyira tells Mayleigh.

"Sounds interesting, I can't wait to try it. You can put it over there next to the other dishes. Make sure to write your name on the card provided so that everyone can know who made it."

"What did you make?"

"My *Plumberry Pancakes* of course."

"Chocolate *Plumberry Pancakes*?"

"You know it," Mayleigh chuckles.

"I definitely have to try it. Your pancakes are soooo delightful."

"You haven't been by the diner this week. Is everything alright?"

"I was unpacking."

"Okay. Well, I gotta go work. I'm part of the planning committee. See you around."

"See you Mayleigh," Nhyira waves shyly.

"Here alone?" Akio calls from behind Nhyira.

"You startled me."

"You look be-you-tee-ful," he drawls. "Glad you could make it out to our little festival."

She looks around. "Little? There are at least one thousand people here."

"Well, what can I say? Chocolate has a way of bringing people together."

"I don't think that's how the saying goes."

"It does in *Njapa*," he smiles. "Did you make anything?"

"My dish is over there," she points to the table.

"What did you bake?"

"*Chocolate Macadamia Cloud Torte*."

"Do you want to cut a slice for me?"

"I thought this was a self-serve kind of festival?"

"Well," Akio stands taller, "I'm allowing your '*self*' to serve me."

Nhyira rolls her eyes. "That doesn't even make sense."

"Wanna go on the Ferris wheel with me?"

"That won't be necessary."

"You say that a lot. Tell me Ms. Enosis, what can I do to become **necessary** in your eyes?"

"How old are you? Do those pathetic lines work on girls around here?" Nhyira scoffs.

"I'm a grown man. I deal with women."

"You're like 18 I'm guessing? Grown? Ha."

"I'll have you know that I am 24 years old."

"Congratulations," she claps. "Why don't you act your age and leave me alone?"

"I'm just trying to be friendly."

"If you say so. Goodbye Akio Qvareli." Nhyira storms off.

"Hey, you remembered my name," he shouts.

CHAPTER 9

"You should be careful with him."

Nhyira turns around to face Mayleigh.

"He has a reputation around town and it's not a good one," Mayleigh continues.

"You don't have to worry about me. I have no interest in Mr. Qvareli."

"That's what they all say, until he lures them with his charm," Mayleigh recounts.

"Thanks for the concern, but guys like Akio aren't my type. As a matter of fact I'm not interested in a relationship. My focus is on my house and figuring out the next step in my life."

"Are you planning on getting a job?"

"I have one."

"You do?" Mayleigh's eyes extend. "Where?"

"Sort of," Nhyira mumbles. "I'm working on a bestseller."

"Oh, you're a writer," Mayleigh replies, intrigued.

"I know it sounds pathetic," Nhyira pauses. "Maybe I should get a real job."

"Do what you love. I love cooking and running my diner. If you want to be a writer then be the best writer you can be. Don't let anyone shatter your dreams. Neither should you downplay it. We each have our part to play in the world."

"I appreciate that encouragement. Can I ask you a question?"

"Of course."

"What do you know about Mr. Veisiejai? The library doesn't have much information about him or his death."

"You should leave that case alone. It's not something we speak about. I'm surprised that you purchased that house. Aren't you afraid it's haunted?"

"Haunted, because someone died in there? I'm not afraid of death, Mayleigh."

Mayleigh shrugs, "I don't know much. The only ones who've been around long enough to know anything about the case is your neighbor Ms. Higüey and the man who lives in that house over there." Mayleigh points to the house Nhyira spotted when she arrived at the festival.

"Do you know his name?"

"Mr. Colafranceschi."

"Who is he?"

"The original Harbormaster of *Njapa*. He was here when Mr. Veisiejai arrived. They were acquaintances. But, he left a year before the **Veisiejai House** was completed. No one knows why. He returned 20 years ago and has been living on the outskirts ever since. His property is private and he doesn't have visitors; only the people who deliver his basic necessities."

"What about his family?"

"I heard he had a wife; not sure what happened with her. But they had no children."

"That's sad, to go so long in isolation."

"His choice," Mayleigh shrugs.

"Maybe I can talk to him. He probably knows more about this case than anyone."

Mayleigh stares at Nhyira. "I don't think that's a good idea."

"Why not?"

"He's an old man. Let him live in peace like he wants."

"Okay then," Nhyira retorts, trying to change the subject. She'd already made up her mind to visit the old man. "I'm going to look around some more. Maybe go on a few rides."

"You do that. See you later," Mayleigh waves.

Two hours later Nhyira begins to yawn. Making her way to the parking lot, she spots a man and woman talking. In passing, she picks up Akio's voice.

She felt a pang of jealousy, but immediately ignores it.

CHAPTER 10

"Leaving so soon?" Akio calls out, as Nhyira walked towards her car.

"Why does it matter? Shouldn't you be with your girlfriend?"

"Girlfriend?" he asks, looking around.

Nhyira motions to the woman standing near a booth.

"I don't have a girlfriend," Akio informs. "She's from out of town; I was answering a few questions that she had."

"I bet you were," Nhyira scoffs.

"Am I missing something here?"

"Look Akio, I don't have time to play any games with you. I heard about your reputation. And believe me I don't want to be a part of your list."

"You don't even know me," he counters.

"Everyone I speak to tells me to stay away from you. Why is that?"

"Who is this *everyone* you're referring to?"

"It doesn't matter. I'm not interested. No acquaintance. No friendship. No relationship. Nothing. Got it?" Nhyira emphasizes.

32 Murder In Zaire Valley

"You should get to know someone before you judge them based on hearsay, Nhyira."

"Are you or are you not the town's flirt?"

"That was High School. Now my focus is on my career. Some people can't get over the past, but that's their issue not mine."

"When was the last time you had a girlfriend?"

Akio peers into her eyes. "Why are you so curious?"

"Nevermind," she turns from his gaze.

"No, it's okay. I'll answer. My last serious relationship was 2 years ago, but that ended badly."

"What happened?"

"I don't want to talk about it."

"I'm sorry to prod. What is it that you do exactly?"

"I'm the Warden for the Underwater Prison in *Kanomatton*."

"You work out of State?"

"It's not that far. That's why you don't see me around much. I work shifts. Have a place out there. When I do come home I hit up **Mayleigh's Diner** and go running in the park."

"I haven't been looking for you. No need to give me a play by play."

"Come on let's go enjoy the rest of this festival, can't have a beautiful woman stand here by herself. I'll even introduce you to some of the residents."

"I was actually on my way home."

Akio takes her hand, "Not on my watch."

"Step right up," a man at the Star Ring Toss calls out.

"1 token please," Akio states, smiling. "I'm going to win you a teddy bear," he blushes at Nhyira.

"That—"

"—won't be necessary?" Akio finishes.

Nhyira laughs and playfully pushes his arm.

Akio winks at her and proceeds to play the game. "First laugh I ever got from you, I'll take it."

"This is for you." Akio hands her a stuffed white jaguar; Starr Islands' national animal. "You can name it **Akio** if you want."

"Keep your stuffed animal," Nhyira declines.

"I won it for you. Please take it."

"Will you leave me alone if I do?"

"I can't make that promise. In case you haven't noticed, I like you."

"Bold statement for a player."

"I'm not a player. Get to know me and you'll see how genuine I am."

"No thanks," she yawns.

"Not used to hanging out late?"

"I should go. I have a long drive home."

"I can drive you home."

"That's alright. I'll get a *Blitz* before I leave. It'll keep me up."

"Come on Nhyira, I can't let you drive home in this condition."

"I've driven home exhausted before."

"I insist," he continues, placing his hand on the roof of her car. "It'll make me feel better."

Nhyira narrows her eyes. "I don't want you getting any ideas."

"It's just a drive," Akio insists.

"And how will you get home?"

"I got a ride to the festival; parked my car in front of the diner. I can walk back after I drop you home."

Nhyira thinks for a moment then offers another option. "How about you drive me to the diner, get your car and then I'll drive myself home. I should be rested enough by that time."

"You're capable of comprise," Akio chuckles. "I'll need your number though."

"M-my number?"

"Yes, so you can let me know when you reach home."

"I'll be fine," she replies.

"I'm not taking no for an answer."

CHAPTER 11

"*Plumberry pancakes* hun?" Mayleigh greets the next night.

"Not today," Nhyira declines. "I want to try something new."

"Order whatever you like, it's on the house."

"That's okay I'll pay."

"No my darling, it's on the house. I insist." She hands Nhyira the menu. "Take your time. Ring the bell when you're ready to order."

For dinner Nhyira ordered *Banana Sliver Rice, Honeysuckle Short Ribs* and the **Mayleigh's Diner** house salad.

"How'd you like the food?"

"Mayleigh, you should be cooking for a huge restaurant somewhere in the city."

"That's what everyone tells me, but I love *Njapa*. I wouldn't wanna cook anywhere else. Let people come to our little town."

"How do you remain so optimistic?"

"God."

Nhyira puts down her fork. "You'll have to share about this *God* someday."

"I'll share what I know. I'm now getting to know HIM myself." Mayleigh begins to quietly wipe Nhyira's table.

"What's wrong Mayleigh? You've gone quiet on me."

"There's something that's been on my mind, I just wanted clarification."

"You're not one to go quiet. What is it?"

"What happened between you and Akio last night? I saw him driving your car after the festival."

"I was tired and he drove me home. No harm done. I slept most of the ride anyway."

"Is that all?"

"Yup," Nhyira nods.

Mayleigh continues wiping the table, "I see."

"What?"

"Nothing," she pauses. "As I said before, be careful…"

Moments later, Akio barges in the diner, walking towards Nhyira.

"Good night Ms. Enosis," Akio states, sitting next to her.

"Mr. Qvareli."

"Why so formal?"

"You started it," Nhyira quips.

"How have you been? You didn't call me. I was worried."

"I'm fine as you can see."

"Why are you always hostile towards me?" he asks.

"I don't know you. Neither do I want to know you," she snaps, rolling her eyes.

"You're going to stay locked up in that big mansion of yours like a *damsel in distress?*"

"Excuse me? If you came to disturb my peace, you can stop right now."

Mayleigh looks at them sternly. "Both of you stop it."

"Night Mayleigh. Thanks again for dinner." Nhyira gets up and exits the diner.

Akio opens the door and calls out. "Why are you running away? I haven't done anything to you."

"Akio please leave me alone," Nhyira pleads.

He stands in front of her. "I'm sorry for whatever I've done to offend you."

She ignores the whiff of his cologne, dancing through her nostrils. "I know you're probably not accustomed to women saying this, but I'm not interested."

He stares deeply into her eyes, unnerving her. "Am I making you nervous?"

"You see that, right there. Stop it," Nhyira contends.

"Honestly Nhyira, I like you. I won't force you to talk to me though. I thought you were a nice person, but I guess I'm wrong. Have a good night." He turns and returns to the diner.

CHAPTER 12

"Good morning Ms. Higüey."

"What are you doing on my property?"

"Can we have a civilized conversation for once?"

Although ready to resist, Ms. Higüey notices the urgency on Nhyira's face and obliges. "You may sit on my bench, but don't expect me to offer you any beverage. You are not my guest."

"That's fine," Nhyira shrugs. "I didn't come here for entertainment."

"What do you want?"

"I want to know about the Veisiejai's. Who were they and what happened between them? How did Mrs. Veisiejai become the prime suspect in her husband's murder?"

"Not this again," she grunts. "That's none of your business, child."

"It is, since I bought the house that they once lived in."

"Speak to your agent."

"You were their neighbor," Nhyira adds. "I'm sure that you know more than Mr. Sellers."

41 Murder In Zaire Valley

"Even if I did, that's the past. Enjoy your new house. If you hear any strange sounds then call the police." She makes her way towards her door.

"Ms. Higüey, please," Nhyira pleads. "If you answer this question I wouldn't bother you again for the week."

"A week you say? That's it?"

"I won't make a promise I can't keep. More than a week seems like a stretch. We're neighbors and you never know what can happen."

"You are nosy."

"Correction, I want to know about the people who owned my house."

Ms. Higüey opens her front door. "Come inside. Looks like the rain's about to burst through the clouds and I won't be catching pneumonia because of your inquisition."

Inside, Nhyira is shocked at the opulence of the house. The house didn't match the owner and she wondered how the old woman kept such pristine décor.

"I know that look," Ms. Higüey grumbles. "You want to know how an old woman like me lives in such a beautiful house."

"Oh I'm sorry. Did my face give me away?" Nhyira asks, embarrassed.

"It's the look that everyone gives when they enter; though I haven't had guests in many years."

"I'm sorry to have offended you."

"None taken," the old woman shrugs. "Have a seat."

Nhyira makes her way to the beautiful Mikado Chaise lounge.

"What exactly do you want to know about the Veisiejai's?" Ms. Higüey prompts.

"Tell me about the couple. How did his wife become the number one suspect?"

"Well isn't it obvious? **Greed**. Poet only wanted his money."

"Did you know Mr. Veisiejai before he got married?" Nhyira inquires, wishing she had her notebook.

"No, he came here with Poet. She was 16 at the time; very immature. You can see that she wanted him for his money. She never spoke to anyone and stayed inside most of the time, except when she hung out with the mayor. They spent a lot of time together when her husband was away."

Nhyira's eyes widen. "Do you think they had an affair?"

"They were quite chummy and he was the only one Poet spoke to in the entire town aside from those who worked in the mansion."

Realizing the woman went silent, Nhyira asks another question, "Was she unhappy, from what you remember?"

"I don't know," Ms. Higüey shrugs, "but poor Mr. Veisiejai loved Poet and would do anything for her. Look where that got him. You should've seen his face every time he'd come back and hear about her rendezvous."

She seems to know a lot for someone who didn't like Mrs. Veisiejai.

"How often did he leave?"

"Because of the house's lavishness he got a lot of the materials from out of State. So he'd be gone for days, sometimes weeks at a time."

"She was probably lonely," Nhyira considers.

"No reason to be. Mr. Veisiejai asked Poet if she wanted to come, but she always said she was the '*Lady of the House*' and would stay to help the servants keep the house together."

How does she know so much?

"I bet you're wondering how come I know all this. Well Nhyira, there were more houses back then. Neighborhood gossip was prevalent. I had my sources."

"Did you ever hear them argue?"

"No. But at night I'd see Poet leave the house from the side door."

A thought crosses Nhyira's mind. "Were you the one from the newspaper?"

The old woman's face falls flat. "What are you talking about?"

"The article about his death stated that an eyewitness saw someone come into the house the night he died."

"I don't know what you're referring to. As I said, there were many other houses back then."

"But your house is at a perfect angle to see everything."

"Did you come here to accuse me?" she barks.

"Accuse you of what?"

"I think you've overstayed your non-welcome. Please leave," Ms. Higüey snaps.

"What did I say?" Nhyira counters.

"I said leave, before I call the police."

"Wait," Nhyira pauses, "one more question."

Ms. Higüey gives her an eye.

"Where is Mrs. Veisiejai now?"

"Last I heard she was in the Underwater Prison in *Kanomatton*."

"Thank you. I'll be leaving now."

"Nhyira?"

"Yes?" she says, stopping just before opening the door.

"I'm not sure what you're trying to accomplish, but the killer's already been caught. Leave it alone. Don't stir up anything in *Njapa*." Before Nhyira could respond, Ms. Higüey pushes her out of the house.

CHAPTER 13

Nhyira takes a gulp of water from her bottle as she wipes the beads of sweat on her forehead. She'd woken up early that morning to run through the park. Living in *Njapa* for almost one month, she drew blanks when it came to her bestselling book idea.

Writing about the **Veisiejai House** was of course the obvious story, but she needed more details.

"Good night Ms. Enosis," a voice booms in the distance.

Trying to hide the party happening inside her brain, she pretends not to hear him.

"Did you hear what I said?" Akio runs to keep up with her pace.

"Oh, hi Mr. Qvareli."

"Can we stop with the formalities?"

"Again, you started it," Nhyira replies. "Haven't seen you around much."

"You were looking?" he blushes.

"Don't flatter yourself."

"I'm pleased to know that someone missed me."

46 Murder In Zaire Valley

"It's not like that," she retorts. "I need a favor."

"Oh, I see." His countenance changes, "You're only speaking to me because you want something. And here I was thinking we were becoming real friends."

"I'm sorry Akio."

"No worries. What's the favor?"

"I don't know the judicial protocol, but I need to know about one of your prisoners."

"How do you know about my prisoners?" he inquires.

"Nevermind that. This is important."

"With you it always is."

"What's that supposed to mean?" Nhyira scoffs.

"Cut to the chase Nhyira. I don't have time for the pretense."

Not understanding his agitation, Nhyira proceeds to ask her question. "Do you have a prisoner named Poet Veisiejai?"

"I do. But, how do you know that? Non-*Njapa* residents aren't privy to that information."

"One of the locals told me."

"What exactly do you want to know?"

"I would like to visit her. Is she allowed visitors?"

"I don't think that's a wise idea. Mrs. Veisiejai is heavily guarded. She's never had a visitor since her arrest in the 50s."

"What kind of sick justice system would leave a woman in seclusion for all these years without **anyone** communicating with her?" Nhyira snaps.

"It was her request."

"Please Akio."

"Why is this important to you?"

"This mystery hasn't been solved in four decades. I live in a house that was a previous crime scene. And the prime suspect is still alive."

"Why are you referring to it as a **mystery?** The suspect was detained. Besides, she's not a prime suspect, she is the **only** suspect," Akio reminds her.

"What if she didn't do it?"

"Leave the investigating to the professionals. They've done their job. This isn't one of your mystery novels," he derides.

"How DARE you!" Nhyira screeches.

"How dare I what? Did I say anything out of order?"

"I really need this favor," she answers calmly.

Akio stands in front of her, a little too close for comfort. "Nhyira, I like you and I've stated this on more than one occasion. However, I think that from now on it's best that we don't communicate with one another. I can't be near you."

"Will you help me?"

48 Murder In Zaire Valley

"No." He runs off, leaving her speechless.

CHAPTER 14

Nhyira knocks on the diner counter. "Did he come in today?"

"Do you like him?" Mayleigh inquires.

Nhyira spins around on the diner stool. "I really need his connection to the prison in *Kanomatton*."

"I hope you're not still on that case."

"I haven't been able to sleep this week thinking about it."

"You need to leave it alone. It's not safe for you being that close to a criminal," Mayleigh reprimands.

"I think she's innocent."

"Of course you do sweetie. But, the officers did their job. Please promise you'll leave it alone."

"I can't." Nhyira gets up and walks to the ladies' room.

"Night Mayleigh, can I have two *Anise Duck Stews* and *Parchese Salads* please?" Akio requests.

50 Murder In Zaire Valley

"Coming right up." Mayleigh calls out to the chef in the back, "Two *Anise Duck Stews* and *Parchese Salads* to go."

"Yes Mayleigh," the chef responds.

"Good night Akio," Nhyira greets when she returns to her seat.

"Hi," he retorts flatly.

Mayleigh's eyes shifts between the pair. "What's wrong with you two?"

"Nothing," they respond in unison.

"Something's going on," Mayleigh notes. "I sense tension."

"What you sense is an inconsiderate woman," Akio counters, glancing at Nhyira from the corner of his eye.

"How am I inconsiderate?" Nhyira inquires.

He looks at Mayleigh. "Do I have to wait long for the meals? I need to get on the road to beat traffic."

"Oh come off it," Nhyira demands. "You know there's no traffic at this time. Talk to me, please."

"You've made it clear where we stand and I respect your wishes," Akio sighs.

"Will you two knock it off?" Mayleigh orders. "Act your age. Here's your food Akio." She hands him the take out containers. "Drive safely."

"You're following me?" Akio asks moments later, when Nhyira stands next to his jeep.

"Akio, please. Please. I don't know why this is important, but it is. I'm begging you." She gets down on her knees.

"Get up Nhyira, it's cold."

"I'd do anything within reason to get just one conversation with Mrs. Veisiejai."

"You're putting me in a tough spot." He reaches down to help her up; an excuse to touch her, since she clearly didn't need his assistance.

"I can't ignore my instincts. I need to solve this."

"Who made you Super Sleuth?"

"Is that a nickname?"

He smiles at her, unable to resist her cuteness. "Okay Nhyira, I'll get you an interview, although it's not a mystery. When would you like me to set up the appointment?"

"If we leave tonight, I should be able to meet her tomorrow morning."

"You mean you'll come to *Kanomatton?*"

"How else will I speak to her?"

Looking at his watch, Akio grins. "It's now 5:30. Do you think you can be ready in an hour?"

"Done. See you then." Nhyira grins, running to her vehicle.

CHAPTER 15

Kanomatton Underwater Prison

"Good morning miss. I'm Officer Cortona. How may I help you?"

"My name is Nhyira Enosis. I am here to see one of your prisoners."

"Oh, you're the one Akio told me about," Officer Cortona retorts.

Nhyira nods.

"Are you a lawyer?"

"No."

"Who are you here to see?" the officer inquires.

"Mrs. Poet Veisiejai."

With his eyes widened Officer Cortona speaks in shock. "Mrs. Veisiejai? Are you a relative of hers?"

"No."

"Then why would you want to see her? Are you a reporter? We don't allow reporters in here."

"I'm not a reporter. I thought Akio spoke with you?"

"He did, but I didn't get all the details. I still have a job to do. Although Akio is trusting… I don't know you," he states, narrowing his eyes.

"Can I just see her?" Nhyira pleads, trying to subdue her annoyance.

"Ms. Enosis is it? What do you want from her? She hasn't had visitors in the four decades she's been incarcerated."

"I have questions to ask her."

"Is this for some kind of school project?"

"Do I look like a school girl?"

"Is that a trick question?" Officer Cortona asks.

"I recently bought the house that she used to live in—"

"You live in the old **Veisiejai House**?"

"You know it?"

"Of course. It's the most popular house in Celgagoas. Davenport has been trying to get that house sold for years."

"You know Mr. Sellers?"

"We went to school together."

"Small world," Nhyira replies, trying to speed the process along.

"Mrs. Veisiejai doesn't allow visitors," Officer Cortona continues. "She wants to live her final days alone."

"Final days? She's not even 65."

"I can't go against her wishes. It's her life."

"Please officer," Nhyira begs. "I promise I won't be long."

"I'll see what I can do. However, if she says no, you'd have to leave immediately. This isn't a social gathering."

"Yes officer sir."

"Be right back." Officer Cortona goes to make a phone call before heading down the hallway.

CHAPTER 16

Icy silver eyes stares at Nhyira. Mrs. Veisiejai was the epitome of beauty; her hair a gorgeous mix of lilac and silver. Nhyira didn't know what to expect, but the glamorous beauty before her wasn't it.

"Who are you and what do you want? I told the officers that I don't want any visitors," Poet declares.

"I'm sorry. I begged to be here."

"Who are you?"

"My name is Nhyira Enosis. I bought your house."

"Why would you want that house? I heard that no one's lived there since the night of my arrest."

"I'm not afraid of the history. It fascinates me."

"Are you a reporter?"

"Reporter? Me? No. I am a concerned citizen."

"Concerned about what?" Poet asks.

"You," Nhyira counters.

Mrs. Veisiejai walks over to the other end of the padded room. "You're concerned about me?" She begins to laugh.

"It's not funny."

"Look little girl," Poet scoffs, "I get your obvious interest in mysteries or whatever, but I've been imprisoned for 40 years. Go live your life. No need to be concerned about an old woman you don't even know."

"I can understand your apprehension, but there's a reason I am here."

"What can that possibly be?"

"I believe that you're innocent," Nhyira blurts, noting the smug look on the woman's face.

"I don't know what stunt you're trying to pull, but I'd like for you to leave."

"I'm sorry. Did I say something to upset you?"

"I don't know you. I don't know what you're doing here, but you need to leave," Poet snaps. "I've accepted my fate and nothing's going to change now."

"But you're innocent and you know it," Nhyira cries.

"The truth doesn't matter. I'm in prison and that's where I'm going to stay until I die."

"But you don't have to. I want to help you get out."

"Leave. I said LEAVE!" Poet knocks on the two-sided mirror. "Guard, PLEASE MAKE HER LEAVE."

"Mrs. Veisiejai, I'm sorry. I only want to help you," Nhyira articulates.

"GET OUT!" Poet screams.

Officer Cortona runs into the room. "What's wrong?"

The old woman with the icy silver eyes speaks angrily. "I don't want ANY more visitors. I'm fine living in isolation. Please escort this young woman out of my room."

Nhyira tries to reach out to her.

"Ms. Enosis, I have to ask you to leave," the officer repeats.

"But she's innocent," Nhyira yells when Officer Cortona pulls her out of the room.

Outside of the padded cell Officer Cortona hands Nhyira a cup of *Cobalt Tea*. "I like your spunk; I really do," he says, "but please understand that this is a delicate situation."

"I want to help."

"But why? You're not a lawyer. Not an investigator. Not a historian. Not a relative. Why does this matter to you?"

"I don't know," Nhyira shrugs, "but it does. I feel a connection to her because of that house."

"If the house is bothering you, maybe you should call Davenport. I'm sure he can find you another house."

"I don't want another house. I want to solve this case."

"All I can tell you is the case was closed forty years ago. Go live your life Nhyira," Officer Cortona pleads. "This doesn't concern you."

"No one cares that a woman is sitting in prison for a crime she didn't commit? She's old enough to be your grandmother."

"I don't make the rules Ms. Enosis. We can't feel sorry for every elderly person in prison, since they committed the odious acts when they were younger. Do you understand what I'm saying?"

"I'm telling you she's innocent."

"What proof do you have? Your instincts?" Officer Cortona laughs. "Go home and enjoy your life. This case has been closed and will remain that way. Please see yourself out."

CHAPTER 17

Akio walks up to Nhyira when she enters the prison's main lobby. "How'd it go?"

Wiping back tears, she sighs.

"What happened? Why are you crying?"

"No one believes me. It was a disaster."

Akio places his hand on her shoulder. "I know you believe that you can help her, but please leave justice to the professionals."

"Who was the professional that put her in here? No trial. Nothing. That poor woman has been in prison for more than half her life and no one in this country seems to care."

"Have you ever considered the fact that she may be guilty?" Akio relates.

"Technology is advanced. Why not open back the case and find out?"

"We're not at liberty to open back cases because some random citizen has a hunch. That's not how the judiciary system works," he replies.

"*Random citizen?*" she scoffs.

"I didn't mean it that way."

Nhyira rolls her eyes. "I get that Mrs. Veisiejai represents a dark part of *Njapa's* history that no one wants to talk about. And here I come, a 'random citizen' wanting to open old wounds. But, I've read books containing cases where police officers arrested any person at the scene of the crime, without a trial, just to say *justice was served*. That's not right."

"I understand that, but this isn't a book, Nhyira. This isn't a story. This is her life. You need to respect that."

"I don't care what you say. I'm going to solve this case one way or the other; even if I have to go to law school."

"You want to be a lawyer now?" Akio derides.

"Mock me if you wish. I can't sleep peacefully knowing an innocent woman is in prison."

"I'm not mocking you, but why do you feel the need to take it upon yourself to solve the case?"

"I don't know Akio. I just do."

"Tell you what. Enough of this doom and gloom talk. Why don't I take you out to lunch? It's your first time in *Kanomatton*."

Nhyira narrows her eyes. "I don't want to go on a date."

"No date. Just lunch," Akio assures. "It'll be impolite of me not to show you the good side of my fair State."

"Just lunch?"

"Just lunch," Akio repeats.

"Nice to see you finally bring someone here again," the Maître D greets Akio.

"Uh, we're not together," Nhyira exclaims loudly, until a few guests give her an eye. "Sorry," she mouths.

"She's a friend. The usual table," Akio tells the Maître D.

The man motions for a waitress. "Please escort Mr. Qvareli and his guest to his table."

The waitress gazes at Nhyira loathingly.

"What's her problem?" Nhyira whispers.

"I have no idea," Akio shrugs.

"Can I take your orders?" the jealous waitress asks, moments later.

Ignoring the woman's obvious annoyance, Nhyira orders with a smirk. "I'll have the *Breaded Hazelnut Pork*, *Parchese Salad* and a glass of *Lavish Lemon Fresca*."

The waitress quickly scribbles Nhyira's order and then turns to Akio, "What about you, Warden Qvareli?"

"I'll have the *Banana Sliver Rice*, *Honeysuckle Short Ribs*, *Whipped Coriander Flatbread* and a tall glass of water."

"Your orders will be out shortly," she mumbles.

Nhyira bursts out laughing. "You have to tell me what's up."

"What do you mean?"

"Our waitress," Nhyira chuckles. "Come on, you know she likes you, right?"

"Didn't notice. She's not my type."

"You have a type?"

"Not anymore," Akio replies. "But I know she isn't it."

"Why? She's pretty," Nhyira giggles.

"I need something more substantial than a *pretty* face," he answers.

Nhyira squirms in her seat, maddened that his words affected her so much. "By the way, what did the man mean by 'again'?"

"Who?"

"The Maître D, when we came in. He made a comment that you brought someone here **again**."

"I used to bring my ex here."

"Your ex?"

Akio nods.

"You brought me to a restaurant you shared with your ex?"

"We're not dating, Nhyira. It's a popular restaurant and I love their food. I come here often."

"Do you cook at all?"

"Why do you ask?"

"Well you come here **often** and in *Njapa* you're always at **Mayleigh's Diner**."

"I love food," he chuckles.

"It's better if you cook for yourself."

"Are you telling me how to spend my time and money?" Akio replies, flippantly.

"N-no. Sorry."

"You apologize a lot. Don't apologize for speaking your mind."

"What happened with your ex?"

"In the past."

"Meaning?"

"Meaning... I don't want to talk about it. Let's enjoy our lunch."

"We're never going to talk about you?" Nhyira laments. "You always have so much to say about me."

"The food's getting cold," Akio replies.

"It's not even here yet."

He picks up a piece of flatbread. "We have this."

"Whatever," she laughs out loud.

CHAPTER 18

Poet looks up in alarm as she hears a knock on her door. This was the second time in less than 48 hours someone knocked on her door during a non-scheduled meal/cleanse time. "Who is it?"

"Mrs. Veisiejai, its Officer Cortona. You have a visitor."

"Again? What's going on?" Poet calls out from behind the door.

"It's the woman from yesterday," he replies.

"She's back?"

"I came to talk," Nhyira announces.

"Is it okay Mrs. Veisiejai?" he asks. "She's persistent."

"Its fine officer, she can come in," Poet replies.

"I'll be right outside," the officer says, escorting Nhyira into the room.

"Thanks Officer," Poet smiles weakly.

Nhyira hands the woman a container. "I brought this for you."

65 Murder In Zaire Valley

"What is it?"

"*Pinkmoon Fries.*"

Poet wrinkles her nose. "What's that?"

"Have a taste. It's really good; got it from the food court across the street."

"There's a food court? I haven't seen outside in decades." Poet looks at her skin. "I must look like a ghost to you."

"You look lovely," Nhyira compliments.

"Why are you back?"

"I wanted to talk. I thought we could become friends."

"I don't have friends; can't even remember how to talk to people."

"You're doing quite well."

"Young girl, I know what you're trying to do, but you're wasting your time. I'm sure you must have a boyfriend or husband and children who you can devote your time to. No need to befriend a criminal."

"I have none of those. Live alone. Have no family. Are you a criminal?"

"I'm here aren't I?" Poet sighs.

"That doesn't mean that you're a criminal."

"According to the law I am."

"Let's change the subject," Nhyira replies. "Tell me about your husband."

"He's dead," Poet responds, bluntly.

"How'd you two meet?"

"That's none of your business."

"Please Mrs. Veisiejai; it'll help if you speak."

"Help who?" she scoffs. "You? In your pseudo-investigation?"

Nhyira tries to reason with the woman. "This isn't about an investigation. We're just having a friendly chat."

"A little personal for a chat, don't you think?"

"When was the last time you actually had a friendly conversation with someone?"

"Before you came yesterday?" she pauses, "Forty years ago when my Kavos was alive."

Nhyira notes tears welling up in Poet's eyes and hands the woman a tissue.

"I'm sorry," she wipes her face.

"No need to apologize. I know you miss him."

"How could I miss someone I killed?"

"Are you admitting it?" Nhyira asks.

"That's what they told me I did. I can't even remember what happened. I blocked out that part of my life. My life is here."

"How did he die?"

"You mean how did I **kill him**?"

"I know you didn't kill him Mrs. Veisiejai. The article I read in the library didn't give the details about **how** he died."

"It doesn't matter. My husband's gone and he isn't coming back." Mrs. Veisiejai begins to cry in anguish.

Nhyira tries to hush the woman. She knew the officer was outside waiting, but she needed more information.

Officer Cortona bursts into the room. "Mrs. Veisiejai, is everything alright?"

The crying persists and he looks at Nhyira. "You have to leave. This is the second time you've come here. The second time she's cried out. Leave her alone. Go home. This prison was quiet without you. We don't want your trouble here."

"I didn't mean to make you upset, Mrs. Veisiejai. I promise to get to the bottom of this." Nhyira reaches out to the woman, but she pulls away.

"Ms. Enosis, leave now or I'll have you escorted to the border," the officer threatens.

"I'm going." She stares at the old woman, "I promise I'll get you out of here."

"Who does she think she is?" a passing guard whispers, when Nhyira exits the room.

"Yeah, those young people are always sticking their noses where it doesn't belong," another guard responds, walking alongside him.

CHAPTER 19

The bell on **Mayleigh's Diner** pings as a man dressed in a sharp gray suit enters.

"Mr. Sellers? I haven't seen you in a while," Nhyira states.

He sits down in the booth across from her. "You've been causing quite a stir Ms. Enosis."

"What are you talking about?"

"I heard that you went to see Mrs. Veisiejai at the prison in *Kanomatton*." He shows the waitress his drink order.

Nhyira immediately remembers that Officer Cortona stated that he and Mr. Sellers were schoolmates.

"News travels fast doesn't it?"

"Why are you bothering that poor old woman?" Mr. Sellers exhales. "Why don't you want her to live in peace?"

"You're talking about **peace** and she's imprisoned?"

"It's not your business," Mr. Sellers snaps. "Is she a relative? Wait, are you related to her? Is that why you're so bent on her freedom?"

"I don't know her."

"Then leave it alone. I'm warning you. The last thing you want to do is get into the crosshairs of the Celgagoan judiciary system."

"Is that a threat?" Nhyira laments.

"I just want you to be careful. You don't know anyone in *Njapa*," Mr. Sellers answers.

"As a resident, it is my business to feel safe. I don't feel safe knowing that innocent people could be jailed. Should I be worried for my safety? Can you have me arrested? Can my neighbor? I know that she doesn't like me. Is that how it works in *Njapa*? Jail all foreigners?"

"You're speaking like a crazy person."

"You think I'm crazy? Can I be jailed for that?" Nhyira screeches.

Mr. Sellers takes a sip of his drink and then stares at Nhyira. "Is that what you think of us, that we would put someone in prison who didn't commit a crime?"

"It's what happened to Mrs. Veisiejai, the woman nobody cares about."

"I'm sure you've heard this enough but, her situation is not your business. We can't change the past. The officers of her time did their jobs and she's paying for her crime."

"A crime she didn't commit. Where is the evidence? How did Mr. Veisiejai die? What do you all have, except a flawed justice system?"

"If you want to solve the case and come up with the same conclusion then be my guest. You're wasting your time." He gets up and exits the diner.

"Are you okay?" Mayleigh asks, after Mr. Sellers leaves.

"I'm fine. I just want to solve this case," Nhyira answers.

"But why? You're not an investigator. This case was closed. Don't open old wounds. You'll hurt a lot of people in the process. It took us a long time to overcome that stigma."

"Stigma?"

"Before we started the chocolate festival, non Celgagoans didn't come here. Everyone was afraid that they'd be murdered or imprisoned for being a foreigner."

"But we're all citizens of Starr Islands."

"Different countries though. And Celgagoas had to overcome the hurdle of being a tarnished country. So please Nhyira, if you respect anyone here, you'd leave the case alone. The last thing we need is for reporters to come flocking from all over the world. As you can see, news travels fast."

"I'll try to do my investigation quietly," she replies.

Mayleigh's eyes widen. "You're continuing the investigation?"

Nhyira nods.

Knowing that she was defeated by Nhyira's persistence, Mayleigh offers a word of warning, "Be careful and remember what I said."

"I will."

CHAPTER 20

Entering her house that night, Nhyira slumps down near the doorway.

Not only was she tired, but she felt the onset of a migraine coming. Hunger couldn't be possible since she'd recently eaten.

Gathering the strength she had, Nhyira decides to make a *Freesia Spice Latte*. The drink would sustain her until breakfast.

She bends to take a blender from the bottom cabinet of the kitchen island.

That's funny. I didn't notice this before.

It'd been weeks since she noticed any indentations in the house. But, this letter was plain as day.

D

She went into full on investigative mode, noting the similarities and locations of the letters.

It'd been the fourth letter she found in the house.

There has to be more letters. I wonder if Mrs. Veisiejai knows about the markings in the house. Maybe she can help me.

Picking up her prized notebook and pen, she jots down her findings.

Case No: 1
Entry 1
Detective: Nhyira Enosis

Crime: Local Construction Magnate found dead in his home 40 years ago.

Suspected murderer: <u>Mrs. Poet Veisiejai</u>
Connection to the deceased: Wife
Location of murder: **Veisiejai House**
Weapon: <u>Unknown.</u> *Details left out of article found in library.*

<u>*My notes*</u>

Mrs. Veisiejai: Seems shy, but confident. Lilac and silver hair. Piercing silver eyes. An innocence about her. Slight immaturity, possibly from decades of not interacting with people.

Possible suspects and motive: ~~Ms. Higüey?~~

- Made several comments about not liking foreigners.
- Also commented on Mr. Veisiejai's frequent absences from the house.
- Spoke about Mrs. Veisiejai's rendezvous with the mayor and her being too young.

- Has direct view of the **Veisiejai House**.
- Comment in article made about caller noting someone going through the side of house.
- Ms. H is the only resident in the area who didn't leave.

IS SHE GUILTY?
Nosy.
Anti-social.

Ms. Higüey?

Motive: Jealousy. ~~She liked Mr. Veisiejai?~~

Other non-related thoughts

Letters found throughout the mansion.

1. Letter I: Living room table.
2. Letter I: Floorboard in main bedroom (where I sleep).
3. Letter E: Cupboard door in main kitchen.
4. Letter D: Bottom cabinet. Kitchen island.

- These letters are strategically placed and spaced out.
- What were these markings for?

- Could these letters hold clues to what happened in the Veisiejai House all those decades ago?
- Was Mr. Veisiejai hiding a secret?

Follow up: Contact Akio Qvareli. Need another visit with Mrs. Veisiejai.

Nhyira couldn't shake the feeling that her neighbor had more knowledge of the crime. What if she was the killer, but framed Mrs. Veisiejai?

Yawning, Nhyira closes her notebook and heads up to her room.

CHAPTER 21

Akio jumped at the sound of his phone ringing. He'd just come out of the shower ready to head to bed, when he saw her number.

Ignoring the blush creeping on his face, he answers in a macho voice; one that didn't sound like a youth heading to bed before 9PM. "Hello."

"Hi, can I speak to Akio?"

"Speaking."

"Do you know who this is?"

"Nhyira."

"I sort of miss you calling me Ms. Enosis."

"Is everything alright?" he replies.

"Why do you ask?"

"You've had my number for weeks and never called me, so I know it has to be something," Akio states agitated. "If it's an emergency call the right number."

"How are you? I haven't seen you around," she continues, trying to soften the tension.

"Spare me the fake concern. What do you want Nhyira?"

"I can't ask how you're doing."

"Great," Akio answers sarcastically.

"Come on Akio, talk to me."

"Look I was just getting ready to—"

"Oh I'm sorry. Are you on a date?"

"Did I say that I'm on a date?"

"I saw the way you looked at the waitress at the restaurant," Nhyira recalls.

"What do you want?"

"How do I ask this delicately—"

"Just ask," he scoffs.

"I was wondering if I can get another interview with Mrs. Veisiejai—"

"NO!"

"You didn't let me finish," she responds, unbothered by his annoyance.

"There's nothing to finish. I heard that you upset her. You've caused quite a ruckus in the prison and I can't have you dodging protocols anymore."

"I didn't dodge anything. You gave me permission."

"Something I now regret. I didn't know you were going to cause trouble. I'm begging you, leave Mrs. Veisiejai alone."

"But she's innocent," Nhyira laments.

"You don't know that. You're wasting valuable time."

"Whose time?"

"The entire country of Celgagoas. Do you want this to become headline news across the globe?"

"If it's a freedom segment for Mrs. Veisiejai then yes, I want this to make global headlines."

"Nhyira listen to me, if I find you anywhere near the prison again, I'll—"

"You'll what? ARREST me? Just like they arrested her? That's what you all do to *foreigners*, right? Silence them?"

"You're blowing this way out of proportion," Akio counters.

"Am I? Am I Akio? You're supposed to be someone who protects the innocent and you won't help me."

"This conversation is useless. I said NO!" Though it hurt him to do, Akio clicks off the phone. One way or the other, Nhyira had to get the picture. This case was closed and it would remain that way; for all of their sakes.

CHAPTER 22

After the phone call with Akio, Nhyira makes her way to the kitchen. She ignores the onset of another migraine. Although it was not her business, as everyone rightfully pointed out, she was in too deep. She'd spend the rest of her life solving this case if that was what it came to.

All those books she'd read of unsolved mysteries or the wrong person being imprisoned, bothered her. She was surprised that all the 'nice' citizens of *Njapa* didn't care to bring closure to the case; even though it happened eons ago.

She began to wipe the kitchen counter of the night's dinner.

On her way to the mansion library, Nhyira hears a noise that sounded like it came from the workers' quarters.

Wrapping a scarf around her neck, she heads to the location of the noise.

"I haven't been in here since the day I moved. Brrrr. It's chilly in here," she shivers as she picks up a few fallen items from the floor.

A sound in the corner makes her jump. "Oh, it's just a mouse. I have to clean in here. Not a fan of rodents," she laughs quietly to herself.

Taking a last glance around the quarters, she heads to close the window.

It's stuck. I have to call someone to get this fixed.

She takes her scarf and places it under the windowpane, attempting to keep the air out.

If she hadn't seen others around the house, she would've missed the letter.

I

This was the fifth letter she'd found. Whoever made the indentations had no preference of location. If it was Mr. Veisiejai, the letters were placed deliberately, a *'Morse code'* of sorts. He clearly didn't mind writing on his prized possessions.

Looking down at her watch, Nhyira rubs sleep out of her eyes.

9PM.

CHAPTER 23

"Ms. Higüey, you startled me." It was a few minutes after 9PM and Nhyira had noticed the woman lurking around her yard. "What are you doing here?" Nhyira utters to the old woman dressed in a frayed plaid robe. She resisted the urge to ask the woman why she dressed dowdy all the time.

"This is your final warning," Ms. Higüey cautions.

"Come inside, it's chilly out."

"I don't want to be in this house," she grunts.

"You've been in here?"

"A few times, years ago."

"I have dinner if you'd like some," Nhyira offers.

"This isn't a courtesy visit. You'll live to regret your inquisitiveness."

"What are you doing at the side entrance?"

"I rang the front door and no one answered. Saw the lights on by the side door."

"I've lived in *Njapa* over a month and you never visited me." Nhyira narrows her eyes for emphasis, "This is highly suspicious."

"Suspicious?" Ms. Higüey squeals. "There you go accusing me again."

"Again, are you guilty?"

"I just came to warn you. I don't care for you, but I don't want you to get hurt."

"Who's going to hurt me?"

"Goodnight Nhyira," the older woman states, walking away in a huff.

Nhyira begins to close the door and spots yet another letter.

H

Okay, now I'm troubled. What is going on here? What are all these letters about?

CHAPTER 24

Guzzling down a *Pineapple Blitz*, Nhyira notes the time on the colossal grandfather clock. 9:40PM. Feeling as if her insides were going to burst she begins to pace the foyer.

"Where would a business man keep most of his documents? Think Nhyira think. Got it... The library."

Tearing apart the library was not on Nhyira's agenda for the night, but she was determined to find all the letters that the carver left. Taking her notebook she starts another entry of clues.

Her search in the library took 2 hours and she'd found four *D*'s.

Nhyira laughs at the random word that came to mind: **FORTY**. Four D's, forty... As in forty years ago the crime took place.

They didn't call her the **Unscrambler** for nothing.

Case No: 1
Entry 2
Detective: Nhyira Enosis

<u>*My notes*</u>

Possible suspects and motive: <u>***Ms. Higüey (MY NUMBER ONE***</u>
<u>***SUSPECT!!)***</u>

- Threatened me on several occasions.
- Came over to my house unannounced using the alleged entry-point of the Veisiejai murder.
- She never visited me before.
- Showing a keen interest in this case all of a sudden.

Motive: **Jealousy**. She liked Mr. Veisiejai?

Other non-related thoughts

Letters found throughout the mansion.

1. Letter <u>I</u>: Living room table.
2. Letter <u>I</u>: Floorboard in main bedroom (where I sleep).
3. Letter <u>E</u>: Cupboard door in main kitchen.
4. Letter <u>D</u>: Bottom cabinet. Kitchen island.

5. Letter <u>I</u>: Workers' quarters windowpane near doorway.

6. Letter <u>H</u>: Right side door of main house.

7. Letter <u>D (x's 4)</u>: Library.

I found 10 letters in all.

Word list from the letters I gathered:

T T E D I H D D D D

1. Die
2. Did
3. He
4. Hid
5. Hide
6. It
7. The

Word combinations:

1. ~~Did he die?~~
2. ~~Did he hide?~~
3. ~~He hid?~~
4. ~~Hidden?~~
5. ~~Did he do it?~~

87 Murder In Zaire Valley

Follow up: Are there more letters around the house? Elsewhere?

- Did Mr. Veisiejai leave clues somewhere else?
- He did build most of the town's infrastructure.

"There's something about this that doesn't add up. Did Mr. Veisiejai know that he was going to die? Better question, did he kill himself? Could I have been looking at this all wrong? Is it possible that he killed himself? Why would a man in his prime - on top of the success ladder - want to commit suicide, knowing his wife would be the prime suspect? Is there a missing piece to the puzzle of their relationship? No wait, wouldn't he out her if there was an issue in their marriage? UGGH!! This doesn't make sense," Nhyira spoke aloud.

Too many questions, not enough answers.

CHAPTER 25

The buzzing of a machine jolts Nhyira out of her thoughts. It was midnight.

What is that noise?

She pulls back the library curtains, rolling her eyes at the sight across the street. It was her neighbor; *mowing* her lawn.

Scoffing, Nhyira grabs her sweater and heads across the street.

"Are you out of your mind?"

Ms. Higüey continues to mow until Nhyira taps her.

"ARE YOU OUT OF YOUR MIND?" Nhyira yells into the silence.

"You're up late," Ms. Higüey greets, nonchalantly.

"What are you doing?"

The old woman mockingly hits her lawn mower. "What does it look like?"

"Who mows the lawn at midnight?"

"I do," she says. "Do you mind?"

"Is this some kind of joke?"

"What's it to you? Can't an old woman mow her lawn whenever she feels like it? I'm sure your big house is sound proof."

"It isn't," Nhyira hisses. "I can hear everything."

"Then maybe you should get earplugs, because I'm in a mowing mood and I'm going to get this job done. So if you'll excuse me…"

Nhyira exhales and proceeds to speak calmly, "If you need help, I can get someone to do it for you, no charge. I'll pay."

"I don't want your help. I've been taking care of my house since I first got it. You're not going to try to dictate my life."

"I know you don't like me—"

"That's an understatement," the older woman chuckles.

"Do you really think this makes sense? You can't even see properly."

"My eyesight is perfect."

"I was referring to the lack of proper lighting you have outside."

"Oh Ms. Big shot with your fancy mansion. Are you **Ms. Popular**, all of a sudden?"

"Uggh, I can't," Nhyira says, storming off.

That woman is incorrigible.

In the background Ms. Higüey lets out a maniacal laugh, as she turns on her machine to start mowing again.

CHAPTER 26

Mayleigh smiles at Nhyira. "Night sweetie. Haven't seen you since last week."

"I've been busy," Nhyira answers softly.

"You hungry?"

"I ate at home, but I'll take something for later."

"No problem." Mayleigh pushes a slice of *Teaberry Custard Ripple* in front of Nhyira.

Nhyira scribbles in her notebook.

Mayleigh glances at the book. "Is this the draft for your novel?"

Covering the page, Nhyira shrugs, "Just something I'm working on."

"Haven't seen Akio either," Mayleigh adds.

Nhyira looks up from her book. "What?"

"Akio, I haven't seen him either."

"Oh okay."

"Now I know you're not pretending that you don't like him."

Nhyira glares at Mayleigh, "Didn't you tell me to stay away from him?"

"He's different around you."

"Doesn't matter," Nhyira shrugs. "I'm not looking for a relationship."

"You can't run from love, hun."

"Who said anything about love?"

"I know what I see," Mayleigh nods.

"Mayleigh, can you come back here for a sec?" the chef calls out.

"I'm coming," she responds. "Nhyira, I'll be right back," she says, running into the kitchen.

"Uh huh. Okay." Nhyira turns her gaze back to the notebook.

Nhyira spent the week looking for other letters throughout the mansion. In total she found **26** letters. Though she was known as the **Unscrambler**, she felt a bit out of practice. Glancing down at her notebook, she focused on the letters on the page.

She made a list of all the letters she'd found…

5 i's	5 e's	2 t's	1 n	1 f	1 w
2 h's	5 d's	2 a's	1 s	1 m	

"Sweetie, its 10:30. I'm about to close the diner. Is everything alright? What are all those words for? Are you having writer's block?"

"Sorry Mayleigh. I haven't heard anything you said."

"Those words. Is everything alright? You know what, nevermind. I'll go make sure they're finished in the kitchen…"

Still not paying attention to Mayleigh, Nhyira continues her puzzle.

These are elementary words. This can't be right.

1. Tan
2. Man
3. Sea
4. Did
5. Die

6. Time
7. Seen
8. Idea
9. Tin
10. Need

Possible sentences:

1. The man at the sea is ~~going~~ to die.
2. I need ~~more~~ time.
3. ~~Will~~ Did the idea ~~work~~?
4. ~~What~~ time was he ~~last~~ seen?
5. He ~~will~~ die.

"I GOT IT!" Nhyira yells, picking up her book and running out of the diner.

"Where are you going?" Mayleigh calls out to her.

I finally solved the puzzle. I need to get back to the prison.

CHAPTER 27

"What ya having?" Mayleigh asks Nhyira, the next morning.

"*Ifeto Waffles, Blossomed Eggs, Plumberry Pancakes,* and a cup of *Cobalt Tea.*"

Mayleigh takes the menu. "That's a hefty breakfast."

"I have a long day ahead of me."

"Where ya off to?"

"Sightseeing," Nhyira retorts.

"Don't lie to me."

"Well, well, well. If it isn't Mrs. Mayleigh Antao," a strange voice utters, interrupting Mayleigh's banter with Nhyira.

Turning around, Mayleigh runs to greet the silver haired gentleman.

"Well I'll be. How long has it been? 3 years," Mayleigh chuckles. "Where were they hiding you?"

"You know how it goes," the man remarks.

"I do," she chuckles.

"Gimme a sec to go wash my hands. You diner's my first stop on this trip. You know I want those pancakes," the man informs.

"Coming right up," Mayleigh smiles.

Trying to hide her obvious curiosity, Nhyira looks at Mayleigh.

"Now where were we?" the older gentleman continues, wiping his hands on a paper towel.

Mayleigh points to Nhyira. "Meet Nhyira Enosis. She's one of our newest residents. Moved in here a few weeks ago."

"Nice to meet you," he utters, offering his hand.

Nhyira lightly shakes the man's hand. "And you are?"

"This man is an important part of our history," Mayleigh informs. "Nhyira meet Corinth Ventimiglia, the very first mayor of *Njapa*."

"One of the founding fathers?" Nhyira gasps.

The man laughs coyly.

Mayleigh hands him a plate. "So what brings you here?"

"Got some business to take care of," he responds.

"How long are you staying for?"

"Until it's finished," he replies, looking at Nhyira from the corner of his eye.

"Always a secretive man," Mayleigh nods in his direction.

"It comes with the territory."

"Well Corinth, I've got hungry customers to feed. We'll catch up later."

"Sure Mayleigh," he taps the counter. "You do your thing. I love what you've done with the place."

"It was nice meeting you Mr. Ventimiglia," Nhyira announces, ready to exit the diner.

"Let me escort you out," he offers.

Feeling uneasy all of a sudden, Nhyira cringes. "No thank you, I can manage."

Ignoring her decline, Mr. Ventimiglia follows her to the vehicle, stopping her. "I know who you are and what you're doing."

"Excuse me?" she snaps, fidgeting with her keys.

He comes close to her ears and whispers, "Mind your business. Leave Poet alone. Don't visit her again."

"Get away from me you creep," Nhyira laments.

When she reaches inside the car, Nhyira exhales a sigh of relief. Pulling out of the car park, Nhyira notes the old man grilling her.

How does he know that I've seen Poet, if he just returned to town? Have people been speaking about me?

CHAPTER 28

Pulling up to the prison entrance, Nhyira notices Mr. Ventimiglia walking towards her. She begins to pick up speed, but it was too late. He blocked her from entering the prison.

"Did you follow me here? How'd you know where I was going?"

"My cousin told me," Corinth grins.

"Mayleigh?"

"Davenport."

"Mr. Sellers is your cousin?" Nhyira gasps.

"My younger cousin. Who do you think got him into real estate?"

Nhyira's heart raced. "What do you want from me?"

"I heard you've been busy," Corinth states, angrily.

"Not that it's any of your business," Nhyira snaps.

"Why are you digging into something that doesn't concern you?"

100 Murder In Zaire Valley

"I find it highly suspicious that you come into town after three years—"

Corinth clenches his teeth. "Look here you twit, we've managed to keep this under wraps for a very long time. The perpetrator is in prison. Leave. It. Alone."

"Are you guilty Mr. Ventimiglia? You seem awful jumpy. Are you afraid that someone would finally find out the truth of what you did?"

"You think I killed Kavos?" he laughs.

"Maybe."

"Why don't you believe that Poet did it?"

"Why does it matter to you what I believe? Besides, weren't you friends with her?"

"We were friends, until—"

"Until what?" Nhyira prods.

"That's none of your business."

"Neither is what I'm doing yours."

Balling up his fists, Corinth exhales, "You should go back home, before you get hurt."

"I'm not afraid of you," Nhyira counters.

"You're not law enforcement, why do you care about this case?"

"I don't have to explain anything to you." Nhyira pauses for a moment. "Wait a minute, when was the last time you saw Mr. Veisiejai alive?"

101 Murder In Zaire Valley

"I can't remember," Corinth replies.

"Hmmm. Wow. Perfect alibi."

"Why would I need an alibi? I didn't do it," Corinth answers.

"Good, then let me find out who did."

He grabs her arm. "THAT IS NOT YOUR BUSINESS!"

"LET GO OF ME!" she pushes him off.

"Is everything okay ma'am?" an officer inquires, walking up to them.

"No, this man—" Nhyira begins.

Corinth puts his arm around her shoulders, "What my granddaughter means to say is…"

"He's NOT my grandfather," she cries, escaping his embrace. "I don't know him."

The officer begins to smile. "I thought it was you. Y-you're Corinth Ventimiglia; the FIRST mayor of *Njapa*. I read about you in our history book. What are you doing here?"

"Nice to know I have a fan," Corinth laughs. "I came to pay my granddaughter a visit," he lies, "but she's upset with me. She didn't get her allowance this month. Kids you know."

The officer nods. "It was a pleasure meeting you sir. Be nice to your grandfather, young lady. You should feel honored to belong to such a legendary family."

When the officer leaves, Corinth returns his gaze to Nhyira. "Now where were we?"

"I was just leaving." Nhyira runs past him.

Safely inside the prison, Nhyira catches her breath.

Is he the reason that Mr. Sellers has been trying to veer me off course? I am adding him to my suspect list. He did mention that Mr. Sellers got into real estate because of him. Maybe he feels eternally indebted to him. He's covering for his cousin.

CHAPTER 29

"Please Officer Cortona. I **need** to see her. I can't stress the importance."

"Ms. Enosis, you're not welcomed here."

Nhyira had been begging the officer for over five minutes to allow her to see Poet.

"But sir, you don't understand," she whines.

"The Warden has asked me not to allow you to see her."

"Akio said that?"

"If you'll excuse me," Officer Cortona states, exiting his office.

"I promise you officer, I won't upset her."

"I don't care. Go home!"

Nhyira runs past the officer down to the lowest level where they kept Mrs. Veisiejai.

"Come back here," he yells.

"Do you understand that this is grounds for arrest, Ms. Enosis?" Officer Cortona announces, when he catches up to Nhyira.

"Then arrest me and put me in this prison. I HAVE to speak to her."

"You're not going to let this go are you?"

"If I end up in this prison, I'm going to torture you with my witty personality," she replies, sarcastically. "Is that what you want, for me to be here?"

Officer Cortona thinks for a moment. "I'm going to ask her, but if she says no you HAVE to leave."

"Deal."

He knocks on the heavy door that led to the prime suspect.

"Who is it?" a soft voice calls out.

"It's me again. You have a visitor," Officer Cortona informs.

"I'm not expecting anyone," Poet replies.

Nhyira sticks her head above his shoulders shouting, "**please say yes.**"

"It's fine. She can come in," Poet sighs.

"Are you sure? Because the last time—"

"I'm sure," Poet exhales. "I can handle it. Anyone this bent on seeing me must really have no life."

"Okay then," Officer Cortona turns to Nhyira. "20 minutes," he says, opening the door. "That's all you have."

"Make it 30?" Nhyira begs.

"Do you want it make it **zero**? You're not supposed to be here."

"I can be, **forever**," Nhyira sings.

"Fine," Officer Cortona exhales. "30. Not a minute more."

"Yes sir, officer sir," Nhyira giggles.

Poet motions to her seat. "What brings you back here?"

"I have something to show you."

"I'm not hungry."

"Not food. I've found some carvings around the house," Nhyira reveals.

"Oh, I'm sorry. I don't know anything about that. My husband took care of all the odds and ends around the house. Any issues with the house you'd have to take up with your agent."

"No, it's not an issue. It's actually essential in helping me find your husband's killer."

"Not this again," Poet rolls her eyes. "Don't get yourself in trouble. I know that this interests you, but I've lost hope about getting out of here, a long time ago."

"Things have changed since 1958. Are you saying that if somehow you could get out of here you wouldn't take it?"

Poet's eyes widen. "You think you can get me out of here? No's ever cared enough for me to even make that attempt."

"Didn't you have a lawyer?"

Poet begins to laugh. "Despite what you may have read about this country's 'advanced state', *Njapa* wasn't as developed as it probably is now. There were no personal lawyers at that time and even if there was, no one would represent me. I was an outcast."

"I'm so sorry."

"So, excuse me if I don't believe in your ability to free me," Poet explains.

"That's okay. Sometimes I don't even believe in myself."

"Why the interest in my case?" the woman asks, solemnly.

"Before I moved here, I didn't know much about *Njapa*. When I saw Mr. Sellers' ad online, I took a risk and it paid off. He gave me the background information about the house and it intrigued me. My house was once a crime scene."

"You are quite peculiar, dear," Poet shakes her head. "What did you have to show me?"

Nhyira digs in her purse for the folded piece of paper and hands it to Poet.

Poet takes the note and reads its contents.

HE WANTS ME DEAD
IF I DIE HE DID IT

107 Murder In Zaire Valley

Poet begins to shake. "Is this some sort of a joke? I don't like it."

"I scoured the mansion looking for clues to this case. Unscrambling 26 letters. It took me hours to figure it out, but it's the only combination that makes sense."

"Why are you showing it to me?"

"Mrs. Veisiejai, answer me honestly, do you know of anyone who'd have wanted to hurt your husband?"

"No, I don't."

"Oftentimes the killer is someone the victim knows."

"I still don't see how this note can help me."

"Do you remember the names of the people who worked with your husband? Or the names of the staff at the mansion?"

Poet rubs her temples, "It was so long ago. I've blocked that part of my life. I'm s-sorry Nhyira, I don't remember."

"It's fine. It's fine. Did he ever have any squabbles with anyone?"

"My husband was a kind man, but he argued with any man he saw talking to me. It could've been anyone he was writing about. He was slightly paranoid at times."

"What do you mean?" Nhyira asks, jotting down notes in her notebook.

"There was this man who worked with him."

"Go on."

"My husband had a business partner. Someone who'd lived in *Njapa* before we moved. He wasn't really that smart with money. Kavos helped him get his finances in order and they became inseperable."

"Do you know where he lives?"

Poet shrugs. "I remember that he moved 2 years before the mansion was completed. Got some job in another country. Kavos was devastated. I don't know if he's back in *Njapa*."

"How was he paranoid?" Nhyira asks, trying to prevent Poet from veering down the wrong memory lane.

"Ummmm, if I remember correctly, Kavos stated that the man was back in town, following him and then vanished."

"Are you sure?"

"I remember my husband's paranoia well."

"Did you ever see this friend after he left?"

Poet shakes her head. "No. That's why I said Kavos was paranoid. None of the workers ever stated that they'd seen him. The man and I were close too, so if he was back in town he'd have come to the mansion. He left on good terms and my husband never spoke ill of him. Only that he saw the man after."

Nhyira smiles, trying to ease the woman's discomfort, "I can see that you loved him; hence why I can't believe you'd kill him."

"But how can you prove it? I don't have an alibi."

"Leave the investigation to me," Nhyira replies. "I just need all the information that you can give me. Anything you can remember will help."

109 Murder In Zaire Valley

Poet thinks for a moment. "I can tell you about the last time I saw him, the day before he died."

Grabbing her pen, Nhyira encourages the woman to tell her story.

CHAPTER 30

1958

"Where are you going? It's late."

Kavos kisses his wife's forehead. "I'll be back tomorrow night. I have to get a new window to replace the one in the workers' quarters; it got jammed somehow."

"Can't you ask one of the staff to do it? It's not a good idea for you to go like this."

"Like what, Poet?"

"Paranoid," she laments. "Didn't you say that someone was following you?"

"Probably one of your suitors," Kavos counters.

"Where'd that come from?" Poet scoffs.

"You think I don't hear about your rendezvous when I leave town?" Kavos snaps.

"You believe rumors, instead of trusting me?"

111 Murder In Zaire Valley

"I don't want to argue. When I return from this trip, we have to speak about a new construction."

"Don't change the subject, Kavos."

Ignoring her plea, Kavos continues, "A new family's moving in from another island. The wife's pregnant and the father wants to gift their daughter a diner. Can you believe it, a baby owning a diner? Of course she won't be a baby when he hands her the keys, but you get the point."

"I don't want to hear it," Poet states, annoyed.

He takes her hands and looks into her eyes. "Are we going to try?"

"I thought you didn't want children?"

"I changed my mind. When this house is finished, we'll need someone to leave it to. I don't want it to rot if anything happens to us."

"Nothing's going to happen," Poet strokes his hair. "Stop talking like that."

Kavos kisses her hand, "Just saying, a legacy will be good. We can have a son or daughter or both."

"Kavos please, you can go in the morning and be back tomorrow night."

"I want to go now to get it over with. This house is taking longer than we anticipated."

"That's because you keep **updating** it," Poet sulks. "Who updates a brand new house?"

"I have a taste for quality pieces and I'm going to furnish my house with the best." His voice changes, "When I'm gone, I want you to stay away from the mayor."

"Corinth's just a friend," Poet replies.

"I had a nice chat with him earlier. I hope he gets the picture."

"Did you threaten him again?"

"No threats," Kavos scoffs. "I told him to stay away from my wife."

"We're friends."

"If he knows what's good for him, he'd stay away," Kavos retorts.

Poet cups his face. "You worry too much."

"I have to protect you."

"I'll be fine."

Holding her waist, he kisses her. "I love you."

"I love you too. Come back safely to me."

"Don't I always?"

Sighing, Poet waves to her husband as he enters the car. She always missed him every time he went away.

Poet looks apologetically at Nhyira. "I'm sorry that I couldn't be of more assistance. That was the last time I saw him," she sighs. "That was the last time we spoke. I loved my husband."

CHAPTER 31

"Tell me more about his friend," Nhyira requests without skipping a beat.

"He had many."

"I meant your husband's business partner."

"I'm sorry, I don't remember his name."

Nhyira gently clasps Poet's hands. "I'll get to the bottom of this, if it's the last thing I do."

"Don't say things like that," Poet grumbles. "That's how my husband ended up dead."

"How did he die? I still don't know."

Poet reflects on the tragedy before stating, "According to the police, he received multiple blows to the head from a saw."

Nhyira gasps, "A saw?"

"Maybe the killer didn't intend for him to die, but—"

"And you have no idea who it could be?"

"It could be anyone. Sometimes we think people are our friends, but they have ill intentions. Kavos always had many people around him; all smiling in his face."

"No one sticks out to you?"

"I have a vague memory of the night. I was the prime suspect because the spouse is always the number one suspect. Some of the women didn't like me because of my age and I was married to the wealthiest man in town. I loved Kavos and would never cheat on him."

"You think the suspect could be a woman?"

"Maybe," Poet shrugs. "I mean, they think I did it, so why not?"

"Tell me about your relationship with Mayor Ventimiglia," Nhyira continues, trying to get as much information as possible.

"To me he was just Corinth, my friend."

"Not so friendly these days."

"You've seen him?"

Not wanting to share about his threats for fear Poet would try to cover for him, Nhyira smiles. "I've seen him around."

"How is he?"

"I don't really know," Nhyira shrugs.

"Good ol' Corinth. I wonder what he looks like now," Poet chuckles softly.

Like a mean old man...

"What kind of relationship did the two of you have?" Nhyira continues.

"Strictly platonic. I can see the question in your eyes; you want to know if there was more to us. Sorry to burst your bubble, but there was nothing romantic going on between us."

"A friendly relationship got you in trouble with your husband? Are you sure you're telling the truth?"

"What reason do I have to lie?" Poet hisses. "I'm already in prison."

"Touché."

"Corinth was teaching me how to read and write properly because my skills were lacking. I wanted to improve my vocabulary and penmanship so that I could assist my husband with his business. That went on for about a year, but it could only happen when Kavos was out of town. He didn't like me hanging out with the mayor. I was young and made stupid choices. I should've respected Kavos' wishes and asked someone else, but I was making progress with the mayor. However, things got weird when he mentioned that my husband threatened him. He didn't take kindly to threats. I've heard Kavos threaten him, but I'd always assure Corinth that it was nothing. The last time I saw the mayor was the morning of my husband's death when he told me that he could no longer tutor me. He didn't want to be acquainted with me anymore. I was upset—"

A thought goes off in Nhyira's head, "Do you think Mr. Ventimiglia could've killed your husband?"

"I don't know," Poet shudders.

"When did you find out that your husband was murdered?"

"I've been a heavy sleeper since my childhood days when I had to drown out the sounds of constant construction at the orphanage. It was no place for children, but we had nowhere else to go. Kavos and I planned on building an orphanage here one day, but never got the chance. I went to sleep earlier that evening and woke up around 8:30PM to get something to drink." She wipes tears from her eyes. "I can't get the sight out of my mind; seeing my husband lying on the bottom of the stairs in the foyer. I couldn't stay and look at him that way; couldn't bear to touch him. It was unbelievable. And right next to the door was the window he'd purchased, blood splattered all over it. I never saw the murder weapon. I remember blood being everywhere in the foyer. Then I heard sirens. Everything was a blur after that. Next thing I know, I was being hauled off in handcuffs."

"You knew you were innocent and didn't say anything?" Nhyira asks.

"No one believed me and the justice system in *Njapa* was non-existent in the 50s. With no friends or proper alibi I was imprisoned. No trial. Nothing. It took me months to even come to grips with his death. The officers tried to make me confess, but I was mute. Eventually, I accepted my fate. If I couldn't live in the mansion with my husband, I'd just die here alone in peace. Of course neither death nor peace came."

"Can I give you a hug?" Nhyira laments, "I know what it's like to lose loved ones. I lost my parents at 14; lived in an orphanage from that age until I went away to University at 18."

"I can't remember the last time I received a hug."

Nhyira hugs Poet and both women begin to cry.

"I don't know why I'm crying." Nhyira wipes her face.

"Me neither," Poet chuckles. "Even if I never get my freedom, I'm glad you came."

"Thank you, but I promise you will be freed."

A knock on the door indicates to the women that time was up. Nhyira smiles at Poet and exits the room.

CHAPTER 32

Akio took a swig of water. He looks up and sees Nhyira waving at him, but ignores her.

Nhyira hadn't realized that things were so tense between them and approaches Officer Cortona sitting at his desk.

"What is it Ms. Enosis?"

"Can I ask you a personal question?"

Fidgeting with his tie, the officer sits up in his chair. "Personal you say?"

"Don't worry, it's not about you."

"Then how is it personal?"

"It's about Akio. I mean Warden Qvareli."

"I don't understand."

"How long have you known him?"

"Have a seat. Knowing you, this will probably take a while," the officer chuckles.

Nhyira sits across from him.

"Do you like him?" Officer Cortona blurts.

Nhyira clears her throat, "Me? No. Why?"

"You want to know *personal* things about him."

"I just want to know why he behaves the way he does."

"How does he behave?"

"Have you known him long?" Nhyira repeats.

"We both went to the Police Academy straight out of High School. From the onset everyone knew that Akio was destined to be on top. He is a driven man and his goal has always been to be the best."

"You don't want to be the best?"

"I like the position I'm in," Officer Cortona replies. "I get to go home to my family every night. Akio on the other hand, can't seem to get it together when it comes to relationships, so he works and travels between States."

"What happened to him?"

The officer lowers his voice, "I probably shouldn't say."

"Please? He's shared how he felt about me on several occasions, but I don't know, officer. Everything I heard about him isn't good. In *Njapa* he's known as a player. Does he have many women out here?"

"His focus is on work. If he shared his feelings with you, that's huge for him. I mean after the last time—"

Nhyira moves her seat closer to the officer. "What happened last time?"

"I'd rather not say."

"You're the only one I know who spends a lot of time with him. Is he a bad person?"

"What do you think?"

Nhyira pauses for a moment, carefully choosing her words.

The officer motions for her to speak up, "Well?"

"He seems distant," she blurts, "kind of guarded. I don't know how to explain it."

Officer Cortona nods. "You're correct."

"About?"

"Him being guarded."

"What aren't you telling me? Please officer. This is important."

Officer Cortona shifts his chair. "I'm only telling you this because you seem to care a lot about him. And even though you say you don't like him, your face says otherwise."

What is he talking about? I don't like Akio...

"I'm listening."

"There was this woman, his ex. She shall remain nameless."

Nhyira sits up, intrigued. "Okay."

"They were inseparable; met back in middle school, friends throughout High School, but he was a player so nothing happened between them during that time. After he graduated, he got his act together and they became an item. Eventually, they got engaged. All was going well until—"

"Did she die?"

"Much worse."

"What's worse than death?"

"She cheated on him."

Nhyira rolls her eyes. "Come on. Really? That's it?"

"Hear me out," the officer adds. "This woman was a top notch lawyer in Celgagoas. She represented stone cold criminals. Men and women whose cases no one wanted to take on. If you were the opposing lawyer in the court you wouldn't want to challenge her. She was ruthless; a force to be reckoned with.

There was a particular prisoner who was weeks away from being released. She had a soft spot for him. No one knew why. One day Akio walked by and saw her kissing him in the interrogation room. Imagine how devastated he was. In his silliness he was willing to forgive her for that indiscretion. But, the man hounded Akio and told him that the woman loved him and they were going to be together.

To Akio's surprise, when the man was released, she ran away with him, never to be seen or heard from again. This was devastating for him and he hasn't been in a relationship since or showed interest in anyone..."

"I-I can't believe what I'm hearing. She ran away with an **ex-con**?"

"Yes," Officer Cortona nods, for emphasis.

"That explains a lot."

"I hope that cleared up anything you wanted to know about him. He's a good guy."

"Thanks Officer Cortona. I'll be going now."

"Safe drive back."

CHAPTER 33

"You're finally leaving I see," a man states when Nhyira exits the prison.

"W-ho— Why are you still here?"

"I told you to **stay away** from Poet. If this case reopens you'll regret it."

"Leave me alone Mr. Ventimiglia, or I'll call the police."

"On what grounds? I haven't done anything."

"You're stalking me."

"What proof do you have, Nhyira?"

"Let me tell you something CORINTH VENTIMGLIA. I'm NOT AFRAID of you and your threats don't scare me. Justice will be served and nothing or no one will stop me from solving this case. So if you'll excuse me..." Nhyira gets into her car.

Corinth stands on the sidewalk gnashing his teeth furiously.

CHAPTER 34

Nhyira was on her way upstairs after a long drive, when a knock is heard on her front door. "Coming," she calls out to the visitor.

"Can I come in?"

"Mr. Sellers, what brings you over here? I'd rather not have you in my house. Let's sit on the stairs."

He looks down at his suit, opting to stand.

"Is something wrong?"

"Why are you still pursuing this case? It's none of your business, Nhyira."

"And **my** business is none of *your* business."

"Look here little girl—"

"Excuse me? Is this how you speak to your clients?"

"You're no longer my client. Just a brat-faced-know-it-all," he snaps.

"You came to my house to insult me?"

"Stay away from Mrs. Veisiejai."

"I'm not bothering her. If she had an issue with my visits she'd have told me herself. Why didn't you tell me that you are related to someone who was an acquaintance of hers?"

Mr. Sellers paces the porch holding back his anger. "I didn't know that I had to explain my family tree to you."

"Why did you tell Mr. Ventimiglia about my whereabouts?"

"I didn't know it was private, since you're going around minding other people's business."

"What am I doing that's so wrong?" Nhyira asks.

"If you think my cousin is a suspect then you're mistaken. You're barking up the wrong tree and a lot of people can get hurt."

"Oh really? Like who?"

"You!" Mr. Sellers storms off irately.

CHAPTER 35

The following afternoon, Nhyira heads to the library.

Mrs. Denoble looks up from her computer. "I haven't seen you here in a while. How may I help you?"

"I need to use the computer."

"Go ahead. If you need me I'm here."

Pulling up a chair, Nhyira takes out her notebook. She types **Veisiejai House** on *Findit.help.* Most of the searches were photos of the house from the fifties to a few days before she purchased it. On the bottom of the search page, she finds a thank you ad from Mr. Veisiejai to the main workers on his house. Four men were listed.

She types in the names one by one. Three of them were listed in the *Njapa* obituaries on various dates. Only one of the men was alive, Rémire Embleton.

Jotting his location, she makes a mental note to contact the man. He had to know about Mr. Veisiejai. Maybe he could explain to her who would have wanted to hurt his former boss.

"Can you believe that lowlife's back in town?" Mrs. Denoble tells a patron.

"I know. And after what he did to Lively. So sad," the raspy voiced woman retorts.

"Who are you talking about?" Nhyira inquires, butting in the conversation.

"Oh child, I didn't see you standing there," Mrs. Denoble jumps.

"Who's back in town? Who's Lively?" Nhyira asks, curiously.

"Ms. Higüey, your neighbor," the librarian replies.

"That's her first name?" Nhyira chuckles. "Thanks for telling me, seemed to have been a secret. Who's back in town?"

"I'm gonna go now. Gotta pick up the kids from the in-laws," the woman informs, walking out of the library.

"My apologies for interrupting your conversation," Nhyira tells the librarian, "but who's back in town?"

"Corinth Ventimiglia, the first mayor of our fair town."

"What does he have to do with Ms. Higüey?"

"Oh, you didn't know?" Mrs. Denoble picks up a paper from the floor.

"Know what?"

"They were engaged."

Nhyira scratches her head. "Come again?"

"Corinth and Lively were engaged. But, that was over forty years ago."

"That's news to me. Why did they break up?"

"Rumor has it, she broke off their engagement when he started spending time with Poet," Mrs. Denoble retorts, walking behind her desk.

"Did they have an affair?"

"I don't know, I wasn't here, remember? But word is, Lively wasn't pleased."

"If they didn't have an affair why would Ms. Higüey be upset?"

"How would you feel if your fiancé spent an exorbitant amount of time with another woman, a younger woman at that?"

"Aren't they in the same age group?"

"Not the point. Anyway, to make matters worse, that pathetic excuse of a man left town to pursue as he put it 'greener pastures'. This devastated Lively even more."

"Is that why she hates Mrs. Veisiejai?"

"That's why she hates foreigners, period."

"Do you think she could've killed Mr. Veisiejai, to get back at his wife for supposedly stealing her fiancé?"

"I wouldn't put it past her. When Corinth returned to town a few years ago and purchased the company in which Lively worked, she retired and stopped communicating with everyone. She has been in that house ever since," Mrs. Denoble adds.

"How could one live their life cooped up in a house?"

"With all the deliveries we have in this town, you don't really need to go anywhere for the bare necessities."

"What about socialization?"

"Not everyone likes people around them, Nhyira."

"I guess you're right."

"Did you find what you're looking for on the computer?"

"Sort of."

"Well come back if you need to."

"Ok Mrs. Denoble, see you later."

CHAPTER 36

After her visit to the library, Nhyira headed to her neighbor's house. "Good afternoon Ms. Higüey," she greets.

"What do you want?"

"I heard your ex is back in town."

"What ex?"

"Mr. Corinth Ventimiglia."

"DON'T YOU EVER MENTION THAT GOOD FOR NOTHINGS NAME AGAIN, DO YOU HEAR ME?" she screams.

"No need to yell," Nhyira squirms, covering her ears.

"The nerve of that man. Hasn't he done enough?"

"You need to forgive him Ms. H."

"Don't tell me what to do. My advice: never get into a relationship. All men are heartbreakers."

"I refuse to believe that. I really hope you forgive him so that you don't die a bitter woman," Nhyira retorts.

"You're a very rude child you know that?"

"First of all, I'm not a child. Secondly, I haven't disrespected you. I just know that bitterness and resentment isn't healthy for anyone," Nhyira schools.

"Hmph!"

"Can I ask you a question?"

"You always have questions," she scoffs.

"Is that a yes?"

"What is it?"

"Do you think it's possible that Mr. Ventimiglia killed Mr. Veisiejai?"

"Why are you still on this subject?"

"You didn't answer my question."

"I don't need to. The killer is behind bars and you need to stay out of it. Goodbye!" She slams the door.

If no one is going to give me answers, I'll find them myself...

Case No: 1

Entry 3

Detective: Nhyira Enosis

My notes

Suspect 1: Ms. Lively Higüey

- Wants me off of the case.
- Failed to mention to me that her ex-fiancé was acquainted with Mrs. Veisiejai. FORMER LOVER.
- Experienced her ex spending time with another woman. Jealous of his attention towards Mrs. Veisiejai.
- ~~Mr. Ventimiglia left her devastated when he left town.~~

Motive: **Jealousy. Bitterness.**

Suspect 2: Mr. Corinth Ventimiglia (**NOW MY PRIME SUSPECT**)

- Acquaintance of Mrs. Veisiejai. Ex-fiancé of Ms. H.
- Threatened Mr. Veisiejai (according to Mrs. Veisiejai).
- Visited Mrs. Veisiejai on the morning of her husband's murder.

- *Left town.*
- *Crush turned sour?*
- *Out of malice he killed Mr. Veisiejai.*
- *Cousin of Mr. Sellers (aka the one who sold me the house). Is Mr. Sellers protecting him? Why?*

Follow up: Visit Mr. Embleton, the only living member of Mr. Veisiejai's construction team to ask what he knows about Mr. Ventimiglia's relationship with his former boss' wife. Find out what kind of boss Mr. Veisiejai was.

Does he have more information about members of the team? Would they have wanted to kill Mr. Veisiejai?

CHAPTER 37

A few days later, with the wealth of information she'd recently acquired, Nhyira boards a plane to Sopr. Vias, the country where Mr. Embleton was said to have resided.

Minoda, Storybook Plateau, Sopr. Vias

Nhyira approaches a gas station attendant. "Hi, I'm looking for the office of Mr. Rémire Embleton."

"**The Boss**?"

"Huh?"

"In *Minoda*, he's known as **The Boss**."

"Do you know where I can find him?"

The attendant points to a building. "You see that house up on the hill?"

"Yes."

"His office is next to it. Can't miss it, his face is on the front."

"Thanks sir."

"You have a good day miss."

The Boss huh? Sounds catchy. Ok where did he say to go? Right, near the house on the hill...

Nhyira rings the doorbell of the office building.

A stocky redhead woman answers the door. "Office's closed sweetie."

"It's only midday," Nhyira notes, looking at her watch.

"The boss is out for lunch."

"Do you know where he went?"

"Home of course. He goes home every day for lunch. What a sweet man. He enjoys spending time with his wife."

"Do you think they'd mind a visitor?"

"They're quite particular about their daily routines. Maybe I can make an appointment and you can come back another day," the woman counters.

"I'm only in town for a few hours."

"Are you interested in having a property built?"

"I just have a few questions," Nhyira replies.

The woman shrugs her shoulders. "Try their house next door. Don't say I sent you." She closes the door on Nhyira.

Ok then.

"Who could that be at this hour? It's our lunchtime," Mrs. Embleton exclaims.

"Maybe they have the wrong address," her husband answers.

"I hardly think this house will be a wrong address for anyone."

Mrs. Embleton saunters to the door. "Who are you and what do you want?" she snaps.

"I'm sorry to bother you. My name's Nhyira. I'm looking for Mr. R. Embleton."

"Why?" the woman glances at Nhyira jealously.

"I'm a Historical Journalist and I had some questions concerning the **Veisiejai House** in *Njapa*, Celgagoas."

"Honey, who it is?" Mr. Embleton calls out.

"A journalist from Celgagoas," his wife replies.

Mr. Embleton limps towards the door sporting a silver cane. "Who are you?"

"My name's Nhyira and I am a journalist."

"How'd you get this address?" he badgers.

"You're a big deal sir, everything's online," Nhyira explains.

"Why are you at my house?"

"I have questions about the **Veisiejai House**," Nhyira retorts, ignoring his wife's disdain.

Mr. Embleton turns to his wife. "Can you give us a few minutes?" He motions for Nhyira to come in the house.

"Call if you need anything," his wife replies, kissing his cheeks.

"You have a lovely home," Nhyira observes.

"I know," Mr. Embleton barks. "What do you want?"

"I'm sorry to have bothered you during your lunch, sir. I wanted to meet you in your office."

"Its fine, you're already here."

"Is your leg alright?" she motions to his cane.

"Fell down some stairs on a project a while back."

"I'm sorry."

Cutting to the chase, he continues, "You're a journalist?"

"Yes."

"What do you want to know about the house? Isn't that information available at the library in *Njapa*?"

"I wanted firsthand data. You're the only living member of the team and I thought you could help. That house is a masterpiece."

"What do you mean I'm the **only living member**?"

"Everyone else is dead."

Mr. Embleton wipes a tear from his eye. "The guys are gone?"

"According to the obits yes," Nhyira nods.

"We were such a great team," he recollects.

"Can you tell me about your friendship with Mr. Kavos Veisiejai?"

"How is **Mr. Popular**? I bet he's transformed that small little town into a megacity."

"You didn't hear?"

"Hear what?"

"He's dead. He died 40 years ago."

Mr. Embleton grips his cane tighter, "I wasn't expecting to hear that. When I left, Kavos was in his prime. Was he sick?"

"No, he died in his house. Blows to the head I heard."

"He was such a kind man; helped me out a lot in my younger days. I'm shocked that anyone would want to hurt him."

"Were you all friends, aside from working together?"

"Kavos and I? Of course. We built most of the buildings in *Njapa* together, long before we had a team."

"When was the last time you saw him?"

"1956 or so. That's when I met my wife and moved here."

"Have you had your business for a long time?"

"Yes. My wife came from *old money* and her father said that if I was interested in his daughter, I'd have to have my own money and a place to put her. So with the savings I had from working with Kavos, I built this house and the office next to it. Business has been booming since."

"And what about Mrs. Veisiejai," Nhyira continues, "when was the last time you saw her?"

"Poet? Can't say I remember. Probably 1956 as well. Kavos and I left town frequently and she didn't have a good reputation."

Nhyira gestures for him to elaborate, "Meaning?"

"I heard she hung out with the mayor when we were gone."

"Corinth Ventimiglia?" Nhyira prods.

"Yes," he scoffs. "Yes, that's him. Cocky guy…"

You don't say.

"Kavos didn't care for him much and they argued about him."

"The mayor?"

"Yes."

"Do you know that Mrs. Veisiejai is in jail for killing her husband?"

"I haven't heard anything about *Njapa* since I left."

"Are you sure you've never been back?"

The old man shakes his head. "I was busy building my life here. What reason would I have to return?"

"I guess you're right. So you've never seen the completed home? Looked it up online?"

"I left that life behind me. My life's here in Sopr. Vias, with my wife."

"Rémire can you help me with something in kitchen?"

"Coming honey," he gets up from the chair. "Excuse my manners Nhyira, would you like something to drink? *Blitz?*"

"No thank you, I'm fine," Nhyira declines.

"I'll be right back."

While Mr. Embleton was fulfilling his husbandly duties in the kitchen, Nhyira begins to explore the living room. She spots a photo of him in front of what appeared to be her house. Snapping a photo, she returns to the seat when she hears someone approaching.

"It's time for you to go," the older woman barks.

"Did I do something wrong? I didn't mean to offend you Mrs. Embleton."

"I don't feel comfortable with my husband talking to some strange young woman."

"I don't mean any harm."

"Please leave."

Nhyira gets up and walks to the door.

"I'll follow you out," Mr. Embleton adds, ignoring the irritation on his wife's face.

"Mr. Embleton, I'm sorry if I caused any trouble. I just wanted to ask questions for my story."

"No problem Nhyira. I hope you got all that you need for your story. But, promise me you'll stay away from me and my family. I don't want any **more** trouble."

"Again, I'm sorry."

"Goodbye." He closes the door behind her.

Walking down the stairs, Nhyira looks up and notices Mrs. Embleton peering out the foyer window.

CHAPTER 38

Kanomatton Underwater Prison

"Your visit here seems to be more frequent than lawyers."

"Nice to see you too, Officer Cortona," Nhyira smirks. "Can I speak to Mrs. Veisiejai?"

"She's expecting you."

"Really?"

"Ever since you left here the last time, she's been more cheerful."

"Good to know."

"You know where she is. The guard will let you in her room."

"I got something for you."

"More food? Another note?" Poet looks at Nhyira's hands.

Nhyira pulls out the recently developed photograph from her purse.

143 Murder In Zaire Valley

"What is it?"

"Do you recognize this man?"

"One of the men from my husband's building team. I can't remember his name, but he was Kavos' right hand man. Why?"

"This is Rémire Embleton aka *The Boss* in *Storybook Plateau*."

"Boss?"

"Catchy isn't it? Do you know who took this picture?"

Poet nods. "I did."

"Do you remember when?"

"No."

"But, you know that you took it?"

"Yes. Kavos wouldn't allow anyone else near his prized saw."

"Why is Mr. Embleton holding it?"

"He only allowed him to hold it that one time, for the picture."

"Are you sure?"

"That I can remember."

"You said your husband received multiple blows to the head with a saw, could this have been the murder weapon?"

"There were many saws on the compound, Nhyira, I don't know. Are you accusing Mr. Embleton of killing my husband?"

"No. This is about the saw. Maybe someone else had access to it and could've used it. Were there any workers around when your husband died?"

"No one worked on the house when Kavos was out of town. However, the house staff did assist me with my chores during the day."

"You need to help me here. Who else would've had access to the house if no one was there and you were sleeping?"

Poet exhales. "If I knew that then I would've told you."

"I'm sorry."

"Its fine sweetie, you're doing your best."

"My best isn't good enough," Nhyira sighs. "I only have two suspects."

"Who?"

"Mr. Ventimiglia and his ex-fiancé."

"Why would either of them have wanted Kavos dead?" Rubbing her temples, Poet paces the small room. "This is too much. I keep seeing my husband lying on the floor and it's hurting me all over again."

"Let's take a moment."

Poet pauses from her gait. "There is something that you should know."

"Go on."

"Only three people know what I'm about to tell you: Kavos, the man in the picture and myself."

Nhyira indicates her alertness.

"There is a secret room behind my husband's desk in his library to which only he and the man from the picture had access. The room contains all of their transactions, blueprints, models of houses, you name it."

"Perfect. That can probably help me. But, how do I get in? Was there a key? Maybe it's still in the house."

"I don't know how they got in," Poet shrugs. "Kavos never told me."

"That's fine. I'll figure it out."

"Tell me honestly, do you think I'll ever leave this prison?" Poet cries.

"Yes, if I can help it."

"I don't even know what fresh air smells like. I'm so pale and ghastly looking."

"You're quite beautiful Mrs. Veisiejai," Nhyira compliments.

"I think this is all I can handle for one day. I appreciate your visit. If you need more information I'll try my best to answer, but not today."

"You've been more helpful than you think. I'll see you later," Nhyira waves, exiting the room.

Case No: 1
Entry 4
Detective: Nhyira Enosis

My notes

Suspect 1: Ms. Lively Higüey

Motive: **Jealousy.**

Suspect 2: Mr. Corinth Ventimiglia (**MY PRIME SUSPECT**)

Suspect 3: ~~Mr. Rémire Embleton?~~
- ~~Mr. Veisiejai's right hand man.~~
- ~~Had access to Mr. Veisiejai's secret room.~~
- ~~Stated he went out of town plenty with the deceased.~~
- ~~Seemed on edge while being questioned.~~

He wasn't in town, Nhyira.

Follow up: Find someone to help me break down the walls to the secret room.

CHAPTER 39

That night, there was only one person who came to Nhyira's mind to help with the search. She picks up the phone and dials the number.

"Hello?" a man answers.

"Akio, it's me Nhyira."

"Yes?"

"I need your help."

"No."

"Please."

"No Nhyira. You've done enough damage and I don't want to be in anything with you."

"What damage have I done?"

"You're disturbing me."

"I'm sorry. I should've asked if you were busy. I didn't mean to interrupt your date."

"Stop assuming that I'm on a date."

"Then what am I disturbing you from? Why did you answer the phone?"

"I'm polite."

"Akio please, you're the only one I trust to help me."

"You **trust** me?" he emphasizes.

"Yes."

"I'm listening," Akio replies, a little more cheerful.

"Can you please come over to the mansion? There's some demolition that needs to take place and I believe two is better than one, to break the walls down."

"Don't touch anything, I'll be right over."

Maybe he does like me... Don't lose focus girl.

"Are you still there?" Akio inquires. "I asked you a question."

"I zoned out. What did you ask?"

"Do you want me to bring you dinner from the diner?"

"That would be appreciated. I'll give you the money when you get here."

"I didn't ask you for money. See you soon," he clicks off the phone.

Why is he being so nice to me?

CHAPTER 40

When Akio arrives at the house Nhyira wraps her arms around him.

"What's that for?"

"I've been treating you so badly and you're still willing to help me," Nhyira explains.

"I told you that I like you."

"But last time I saw you at the prison, you ignored me."

"Perception. My mind was far. I'm sorry," Akio apologizes.

"Care to share? What happened?"

"They want to expand the Underwater Prison to include criminals from other countries."

"Why?"

"I don't know. They asked for my opinion, but I'm conflicted. I think Starr Islands should be a safe haven to help people. I don't think expanding a prison would do that. Parents need to teach their children proper behavior at home."

"You want children?" Nhyira inquires.

"Someday."

"So you **do** want to get married?"

"You think I don't?"

"It's just that—"

"Oh," he lowers his voice, "I guess you heard about my ex."

"Sorry."

"No need to apologize. It's in the past." He holds up a sledgehammer. "Ready?"

"Ready," Nhyira echoes.

"Are you seeing what I'm seeing?" Akio brushes dirt off his clothes.

"It's like a mini city in here. When did Mr. V have time to build all of this? It's so advanced looking."

"Nhyira there has to be millions of dollars' worth of items in here. Where'd he get all of this?"

"He was known to travel."

"Do you think he stole it?"

"No I don't. Come look at this. This closet labeled **Blueprints**. Could this have been what Mr. Embleton was talking about?"

151 Murder In Zaire Valley

"Mr. Embleton?"

"One of the men on Mr. Veisiejai's team made a comment about Mr. V building a *megacity*. Look around you; this is a model for a huge city. What if the killer was trying to get their hands on these blueprints and this model?"

"That is motive," Akio nods. "The builder would've been rich beyond imagination."

"I've been living here for months and didn't know there's a gold mine right under my nose."

Akio rummages through the closet. "All of these prints have two names on them '**K. Veisiejai** and **R. Embleton**'."

"They were business partners."

"Do you think Mr. Embleton could've done it?"

"He wasn't in the country. It is a possibility though. But, who knows. Ms. H and Mayor Ventimiglia are my prime suspects," Nhyira adds, scanning the room for more clues.

"I may be the Warden, but mysteries are your territory."

The room suddenly felt small. Could it be possible that she was attracted to Akio?

"Is something wrong?"

"Nope," Nhyira says, backing up onto a desk. On top of the desk she finds what looked to her like a journal. She flips through the pages and then gasps. "Akio look. It's the exact words that I created based on the letters I found around the house."

"What words?"

She hands him the journal.

He wants me dead.
If I die, he did it.

"There's more. You should keep reading," Akio informs, handing her back the journal.

Nhyira's eyes scans over the words. "This '**he**' was following Mr. V. There are several entries stating '*he's following me.*'"

"You know what that means?"

"That the killer is a **he**?"

Akio shrugs, "I was going to say that he had a stalker."

"You don't think this is evidence?"

"I think you'll need more than a journal and secret room to find the killer."

Is he mocking me?

CHAPTER 41

"I'll see you around." Akio hugs Nhyira, as he opens the door to leave.

They hadn't noticed Ms. Higüey sulking at the entrance.

Nhyira smiles at the old woman. "Good night Ms. Higüey, to what do I owe the pleasure of your visit?"

"Have you no shame?"

Akio exits the house, leaving the two women to their squabble.

"Would you like to come in?" Nhyira offers.

"I think you've had enough visitors," the woman motions toward Akio. "You should be ashamed of yourself."

Nhyira rolls her eyes. "What do I need to be ashamed about?"

"A young single woman like you with a man in your house, it doesn't look good."

"How is that any of your business?"

"Every time he comes here there's so much noise. Sounded like hammers and falling concrete."

"You're quite inquisitive, coming over here more often. Maybe one day we can have a meal together."

"I doubt that I'll ever be in this house again. What is going on between you and that boy?"

"I'm sorry, you're not my mother. This isn't your house."

"Clearly you have no respect for yourself."

"Excuse me?" Nhyira scoffs.

"You shouldn't allow all manner of **men** to be in your house, especially not at this hour. That's how Poet got in so much trouble."

"I think you were jealous of her."

"You weren't there. You didn't see what I saw."

"Either way, you need to mind **your** business. Akio being in my house is mine."

"Have it your way. Just keep your late night rendezvous to yourself," Lively snaps.

"It's not even 7PM yet. Anyways, you have a good night."

Disregarding her neighbor's random visitation, Nhyira writes down her latest entry in her notebook. She couldn't ignore the feeling that she was missing an essential piece of evidence.

Case No: 1

Entry 5

Detective: Nhyira Enosis

My notes

Suspect 1: Mr. Corinth Ventimiglia (**MY PRIME SUSPECT**)

Suspect 2: Mr. Rémire Embleton? *Maybe...*

Thoughts:

According to Mr. Veisiejai's journal, the killer is a **male**. That only leaves two men: Mr. Ventimiglia and Mr. Embleton. But, only one of them was seen on the day of the crime.

Could there be someone else that I overlooked?

CHAPTER 42

The next morning Nhyira's body ached from the tossing and turning she'd done the night prior. She placed *Rain Bread* in the oven to eat with melted cheese and poured herself a cup of *Cobalt Tea*.

Throughout the night the name **Colafranceschi** rang in her mind. He had to know something. Being the town's previous Harbormaster meant that he would know who came in and out of *Njapa* via waterway.

Maybe he could tell her about the day of Mr. Veisiejai's murder.

Nhyira quickly dials Akio's number.

"Good morning Ms. Enosis."

"Mr. Qvareli."

"You sound tired."

"I didn't get any sleep last night."

"Thinking about me?"

"Don't flatter yourself," Nhyira laughs, taking a sip of her tea.

"I know you only call when you want something. What is it this time?"

"If that's what you think of me, why do you bother answering my calls?"

"Because I like you. I love hearing your voice."

Nhyira tries to control the blush on her face. "Um, have you had breakfast yet?"

"Why? Did you want to go on a breakfast date with me?"

"I wanted to make you breakfast as a thank you for helping me yesterday."

"It was my pleasure. Now what is it that you called me for?"

"There's this man—"

"Hold on, you're calling to ask me advice on you dating someone else?"

"Jealous?"

"I won't help you. Why are you laughing?"

"You're always telling me about jumping to conclusions and that's exactly what you're doing now."

"I don't want to talk about another man with you," Akio mumbles.

"We're not dating, why does it matter?"

"Only because you're beautiful I won't hang up."

"You think I'm beautiful?"

"Of course," Akio answers.

Clearing her throat, Nhyira continues. "The reason for my laughter is…"

"I'm listening."

"You have it all wrong."

"What do I have wrong?"

"The man I'm speaking about is an old man."

"Oh, so you're interested in older dudes? That's even worse."

"Akio just stop."

Although she didn't mind the banter with Akio, she had to focus on the reason for her call.

What is happening to me? Since when does he make me blush?

"Do you know Mr. Colafranceschi?"

"The man who lives on the other side of the beach? What about him? You know he's **way too old** for you right?"

"Akio, will you listen?"

"I am."

"I want to speak to him about the case. Do you want to come with me? I think he can help."

"I heard he doesn't like visitors, sort of like your neighbor."

"We can at least try."

"I haven't agreed."

"Please Akio Qvareli."

"My full name," he pauses. "Fine, only because I like you. I'll be there in an hour."

"Thank you much."

As soon as she hung up the phone, Nhyira ran to the bathroom to get ready. This wasn't a date, but now that the thought of Akio made her blush, she needed to ensure that she looked less homey.

CHAPTER 43

"All that for an old man?" Akio smirks, looking her up and down.

"Are you ready?"

"We can take my car."

"No thanks," Nhyira declines. "I want to be able to escape if I need to."

"Escape from what?"

"Well we do live in a town with a murderer on the loose," Nhyira laughs.

"That's not even funny."

"We can take your car Akio. Let's go."

"Have you ever been to this part of town before?"

"No. Have you?"

"Spent most of my life in *Njapa*, but I've never been here. Do you have a game plan?"

"A what?"

"Game plan. Do you know what you're going to say to him? You can't just show up at his front door asking questions about a dead man."

"I have my ways of finding things out."

"When are we going to stop playing these games and go on a date?" Akio blurts.

"I'm not interested in dating."

"You can't tell me that you don't like me."

"Watch the road," she points.

"My eyes are where I want it to be," Akio grins.

"So you want to get into an accident to prove a point?"

"I'm a careful driver. How about that date?"

"Um, looks like we're here." She unbuckles her seatbelt and hops out of the vehicle.

Mr. Colafranceschi opens the door, a few minutes later.

Hmmmm. Don't he look spiffy?

The old man was wearing a mint condition 1920s varsity jacket. Definitely not what Nhyira expected.

"Hi. Are you Mr. Colafranceschi?"

"Who wants to know?" the feisty old man retorts.

"My name's Nhyira Enosis."

"I like your name." He looks at Akio. "Is this your boyfriend? Husband?"

Akio extends his hand to the gentleman. "Akio Qvareli," he says, introducing himself.

The man shakes Akio's hand. "What brings you two on my property?"

"We're here to see if you can help us solve a murder," Nhyira informs.

"A murder huh? Intriguing. Come in."

"Your house is incredible sir," Nhyira commends, once inside.

"Call me Reggio," the old man corrects.

Nhyira shakes her head. "I'll stick with Mr. C or sir."

"Suit yourself. Care for something to drink?"

"No thank you."

He looks at Akio.

"What the lady said."

"Have a seat." He points to a nearby sofa. "A murder you said huh? Whose murder?"

"Mr. Veisiejai."

The old man's countenance changes. "Haven't heard that name in a while. What about the murder, I thought his wife was convicted?"

"Do you believe she did it?" Nhyira asks, flipping open her notebook.

"I wasn't around town when it happened. But, I do remember an innocent girl. Pleasant. Always smiling in spite of how the locals treated her," Reggio recounts.

"I moved into the **Veisiejai House** a few months ago and discovered some carvings on the furniture and other items in the house that has led me to believe that Mrs. Veisiejai was framed."

"You don't say," Reggio replies. "Are you a detective?"

Akio smiles at Nhyira. "She's just a really curious citizen."

Mr. Colafranceschi looks at the duo. "You know what they say about curiosity."

"That phrase doesn't scare me," Nhyira counters.

"How can I help?"

"Do you have any trip/visitors log books in your house?"

"Gave most of that stuff away when I moved, but, I think I may have one left. Hold on." He leaves the room and heads upstairs.

Nhyira sighs.

Akio takes her hand and squeezes it. "It's going to be fine. I know you'll solve the case."

"You think so?"

"I do."

"Thanks." She pulls her hand away from him, turning her head to hide the smile.

"Are you okay?" Akio inquires.

"Uh huh," she shrieks.

Mr. Colafranceschi returns. "Here. This is all I have."

"What is it?"

He hands Nhyira the huge book. "It's the log from my first year as Harbormaster; dated 1953."

"This is perfect. I'm not sure what I'm looking for, but I believe it can help."

He walks towards the door. "I'm due for a midday rest in a bit. Do you think you can wait outside until I wake up? Maybe drive up the road, there's a café where you both can have lunch. Come back with the book when you're done."

Taking the hint, Nhyira nods. "Sure. Thank you. We'll be back around 4-ish?" she says, as they head to the door.

"Good timing." He waves to them as they drive off.

CHAPTER 44

Akio calls the waiter over.

"Yes sir?"

"Can I get a to-go box for this cake?"

"We can give you a fresh slice if you'd like, on the house," the waiter offers.

"Thanks. And bring the check please."

"No problem," the waiter replies.

Akio turns his gaze back to Nhyira. "Found anything?"

Looking up from the book, Nhyira exhales. "Nothing. Just names and more names. Not one Mr. Veisiejai."

"Keep looking, I'm sure it'll pop up."

Drinking her *Passion Fruit Blitz*, Nhyira's fingers scrolls down the page. Just then she spots **Kavos Veisiejai**. "Akio, I found his name."

"See, I told you."

She traces her fingers across the lines and sees **Poet Veisiejai** listed underneath *Spouse*, and then she stops.

It can't be. This isn't possible...

A tear falls from her eye.

"Here you go sir," the waiter says, handing Akio a box. "Have a great day. Do come back."

Without a second thought, Nhyira runs out of the café crying hysterically.

CHAPTER 45

Moments later, Akio spots Nhyira leaning against his jeep with a tear stained face. He walks up to her and puts his arm around her shoulders. When she doesn't push him away, he allows her to place her head on his shoulder. "What's wrong? What did you see?"

"Where's the book?"

He shows her the book, "Right here."

"Read what it says next to Mr. Veisiejai's name."

Akio skims to the names listed next to **Kavos Veisiejai**.

Visitor Name	Spouse Name	Country of Origin	Next of Kin
Kavos Veisiejai	Poet Veisiejai	Grape Fjord, Mt. Thafivin	Kedro Enosis (Brother)

"Why does Mr. V's *Next of Kin* have your last name?" Akio asks.

"That's my grandfather's name," she laments. "If this log is accurate, it means that Mr. Veisiejai is my **great-uncle**."

Akio's eyes widen. "Wow. What are you going to do?"

"I have to go back home."

168 Murder In Zaire Valley

"To the mansion?" Akio asks.

"Mt. Thafivin."

"Do you want me to come with you?"

"You have a job to do," Nhyira declines. "Besides, I think I need to do this on my own."

CHAPTER 46

Grape Fjord Historical Archives

Nhyira hadn't expected to return to *Grape Fjord*, especially not under these circumstances. But, she needed answers. The log book from Mr. Colafranceschi was only a piece of the puzzle. She needed historical evidence to back up her theory that she was related to Kavos Veisiejai.

After they left the café, Nhyira and Akio gave Mr. Colafranceschi his log book and thanked him for his assistance. She decided to keep her possible relation to the deceased to herself for fear that news spread around town, creating an even bigger controversy.

Getting to the bottom of this mystery was her top priority.

There were many names listed in the **V Section** of the archives. Finally, she found a book marked **1930s Births and Deaths**. She looked for her grandfather's name.

Nhyira wipes the tears from falling on the tattered book. Taking out her camera, she snaps pictures of the pages containing her family history.

As she read through the remaining pages of the document, Nhyira holds her head trying to grasp all that she'd discovered.

Grape Fjord Public Records			
Name	Parents	Siblings	Location
Kedro Enosis (January 28, 1930) Death **1970**	N. Enosis (Mother) (Birth date unknown, 1912) Death **1938** K. Enosis (Father) (Birth date unknown, 1912) Death **1931**	Kavos Veisiejai (Brother) (**Addendum:** Through mother's remarriage to G. Veisiejai) (January 30, 1932) **Death Unknown**	Grape Fjord, Mt. Thafivin

Not only was she close to solving a 40 year old crime, but the house she currently lived in, once belonged to her long lost deceased great-uncle. That meant the woman sitting in jail for 4 decades was her great-aunt by marriage. She had a living relative.

This is insane. Like colossal data just dropped into my lap.

"Mr. Veisiejai is my great-uncle? Someone killed my uncle. Breathe Nhyira, breathe. I have to find his killer. This has opened up a new chapter in my life. Is this why I felt a connection to the house? Is this why I needed to solve the crime, to find the pieces of my family history I never knew existed?" She wipes tears from her eyes.

171 Murder In Zaire Valley

"Shhhhh," a patron sitting on a nearby chair, hushes.

"**Sorry**," Nhyira mouths, trying to stand up. She needed fresh air and fast.

CHAPTER 47

Exiting the library, Nhyira bumps into a woman.

"Are you in a hurry?"

"I'm sorry ma'am—" Nhyira begins to apologize until she recognized the woman. "Hi, Mrs. Oberhaus."

The woman peers over her spectacles at Nhyira. "Why if it isn't **The Unscrambler** herself. How are you darling?" The woman hugs her.

Mrs. Oberhaus was one of the oldest women in *Grape Fjord*. At 94 years old, she was also the local Historian.

"I'm doing well."

"You live in Celgagoas now, right?"

"Yes."

"Do you like it there?"

"It's different, found myself tangled in a situation."

She motions for Nhyira to sit, "Ohhhh, do tell."

"I was just on my way out."

"I haven't seen you in a long time, the least you can do is give an old woman a few minutes of your time."

"Yes, ma'am," Nhyira nods.

"What brings you back home?"

"I need historical data."

"Did you check the archives?"

"I did, but I need confirmation."

"I'm all ears. Ask away."

Nhyira explains her ordeal to the woman.

"You've asked the right person. I know all about your family. I thought you knew."

"I don't know anything," Nhyira laments.

"Oh yes, that's right. Your grandparents died before you were born."

Nhyira nods. "Can you please tell me about my history?"

"Of course honey," Mrs. Oberhaus smiles. "Your grandfather's brother was an adventurous chap. He was not one to stay anywhere for long. I'm surprised you don't know this story."

"My parents never shared my ancestry with me."

"So everything's been a mystery to you?"

"Yeah. Until now. Can you tell me what you know about my family?"

The old woman nods.

Nhyira inclines her ears towards the story.

"When Kavos met his wife she was a 16 year old orphan. It was the talk of the town: rich marrying poor. Your grandfather detested the idea that his brother would marry beneath their status and refused to meet Poet. He had control over Kavos' inheritance until he turned 25, but Kavos did not want the money, so he left with his wife and never returned. He chose love over money. Kedro never spoke of his brother to anyone in town. Quite a sad story if you ask me."

"My uncle didn't leave on good terms?"

"They were two hard-headed boys. Lost their mother early and didn't know how to deal with it. That poor woman had it tough. Lost her first husband at sea, he was a Sea Captain. She quickly remarried and sadly lost her second husband - a wealthy man - to pneumonia sometime after Kavos was born. His exact date of death is unknown. A neighbor raised the boys until they were old enough to venture out on their own.

For your grandfather that was age 14. He took his brother with him and they traveled around until he convinced men to help them build a house. Years passed and life was good for the brothers. Your grandfather married and his brother continued in his travels. When Kedro heard of Poet he forbid your uncle to be with her, but Kavos was in love," Mrs. Oberhaus reveals. "And here you are 40 years later in the very house that your uncle built. This is a fascinating story. Maybe you should write a book about it. You're still into writing aren't you?"

"You remember a lot."

"Anything that's historical is my business," Mrs. Oberhaus smiles. "I hope you visit more often. I'm happy to see you."

"I'll try, but my life's in *Njapa* now."

"Never forget where you came from."

"How can I forget *Grape Fjord*? I'm a legend here," Nhyira chuckles.

The old woman begins to laugh.

"I really appreciate this information, Mrs. Oberhaus."

"You're welcome. By the way, my great-grandson asked about you the other day."

"Me? Why?"

"You know he's always had a crush on you since you were in daycare together."

"Tell him that I said hi."

"I'll tell him. Maybe he can visit you in *Njapa* sometime."

"I wouldn't say no to a visit from a familiar face. It's time for me to head back. Thanks again Mrs. Oberhaus."

"You're welcome dear."

CHAPTER 48

Kanomatton Underwater Prison

Akio runs up to Nhyira the next morning. "I'm glad to see you."

"Yeah, you're coming here more often," Officer Cortona smirks.

"I got the information," she whispers to Akio.

Akio joins her stroll to Mrs. Veisiejai's room. "Did you confirm your theory?"

Nhyira nods.

"How do you think she'll take the news?"

"I don't know," Nhyira shrugs. "I'm just going to be straight up with her."

"Want to join me for dinner later?"

"I can't. Not dating anyone. I'm sure you'll find someone else. Please excuse me."

Akio glances at Nhyira, notes her seriousness and saunters away.

"Good morning, Nhyira."

"Good morning, Mrs. Veisiejai."

"What's that look on your face?"

"I have something to tell you, but I don't know how you'll take it."

Poet exhales, "I knew it."

"You do?"

"You can't get me out of jail. Thanks for trying Nhyira. It was great having your company all these weeks. For a moment there I thought— Ah well, my life will go on, even though it'll be in this ill begotten prison cell."

"I'm still working on your case. That's not the news I have."

"What is it then?"

Nhyira hands Poet the pictures she took from the Harbormaster's log book and the *Grape Fjord* archives. "Notice anything?"

"My husband's name?"

"Look again."

"I don't understand."

"The other names in the photos."

"His brother?"

"Exactly."

"Exactly what?"

"The last name... **Enosis**."

"And? W-wait a minute... That's your last name."

"EXACTLY!"

"What does this mean?"

"Kedro Enosis was my grandfather."

Poet looks at Nhyira stunned.

"My grandfather and your husband were brothers."

"Then that means—"

"I'm your great-niece," Nhyira finishes.

"How is this possible?"

"The facts are all there. I got it confirmed by a historian who informed me the details are accurate."

"I have to sit down," Poet breathes.

"You are sitting, Mrs. Veisiejai."

"I have a niece?"

"Yes," Nhyira responds tearfully.

"Don't cry. You're going to make me cry."

"I can't help it," Nhyira sniffles.

"I have a niece. I have family. *A living relative*," Poet sobs.

"I'm going to find my uncle's killer."

"I have a niece. I have a niece," Mrs. Veisiejai continues excitedly.

"Yes and I'm right here."

"Now that I see your face, you do like Kavos' mother."

"Oh wow. I don't even know what my ancestors look like. Did you have photos?"

"I think there's an album in Kavos' library. There are pictures of his parents and older brother. They didn't have the best relationship, but he respected his brother."

"I'll have to look for the album. In the meantime, I'm going to get you out of here."

"Knowing that I have family is the best news you can give me."

"Tell me that when you're on the outside. Oh look at the time, I should be going now. Have a stop to make before I return home."

"I guess I'll see you then? *Niece.*"

"Yes aunty, you will. Sleep well. Soon enough you'll be sleeping on your own bed." Nhyira hugs the woman, tighter than before.

I have family...

CHAPTER 49

Nhyira puts down the sun visor as the midday sun beamed through the windowpane of her vehicle. Just then, her favorite song came on the radio.

Cranking it up, she begins to sing on top of her lungs. Today was going to be a great day and she wanted the world to know it.

"…I'll always have those prettyyyy memorieeeessss."

She hadn't given thought to telling Akio bye when she left the prison. The excitement was too real for her and she wanted to catch Mr. Colafranceschi before lunch.

The time was now 12:10 and she knew that Mr. C would be taking his noonday nap, but she couldn't resist the urge to ask him one more question. 4 months had passed since she moved to *Njapa* and things couldn't have been more promising. She was about to make an old woman's dream come true.

Reggio hides his eyes from the sun's glare. "Nhyira?"

"My apologies for disturbing your naptime sir, but I need one more piece of information for my case."

"Can it wait?"

"No sir."

"Come in, come in. Where's your boyfriend?"

"Akio's not my boyfriend. He's at work."

"I can see that you two like each other. Don't wait too long," he advises. "Never miss out on a chance at true love."

"I don't know what you folks see. There's no like or love between Akio and I."

"Maybe not for you, but that boy's crazy about you."

"Can I ask my question?"

"Yes, go ahead."

"Where can I find the visitors logs for the years 1956-1958?"

"Very specific years."

"It's helpful to narrow things down," Nhyira replies.

"I don't have any more books. As I said, I gave them away. But, if I remember correctly, the log books are placed in the library's archives at the end of each year. I know everything is digital now, so I don't know if they'd still have the originals."

"I think they will. Thanks Mr. C. You have been a tremendous help."

"Well, be sure to include me in your book's dedication," he chuckles.

"Who said I was writing a book?"

"Oh you will. I just know it."

"Thanks again sir. See you around."

"Bye Nhyira."

I guess I'm heading to the library.

Nhyira hadn't noticed the missed call on her phone. It was Akio. A smile crept across her face. Taking a sip of her *Grape Blitz*, she reverses from Mr. Colafranceschi's driveway. "Time to bring this case to an end."

*Sorry Akio, nothing personal. I can't do this with you. Whatever it is that you **think** we have going on. Family's more important.*

CHAPTER 50

It was now 5PM and Nhyira's stomach gurgled from hunger. She hadn't eaten since breakfast, but couldn't stop looking through the books. There were a total of 12 log books from the years 1956-1958 in the library's archives. Who knew *Njapa* was a bustling city in the 1950s?

"Are you hungry?" Mrs. Denoble asks, bringing Nhyira a slice of *Teaberry Custard Ripple*.

"Oh wow, you read my mind. Thanks," she says, taking a bite of the dessert.

"You've been in this room for hours."

"I feel like I'm making progress."

"Need any help?" Mrs. Denoble asks.

"You have patrons to take care of. I'm good. Thanks," Nhyira declines, politely.

"Okay. Well if you're hungry or thirsty, we have refreshments in the lunchroom. It's Staff Day. Help yourself."

"I'm not staff."

"But, you're a special patron and I appreciate you. We don't get much youth in the library."

"I'm glad that I can be a pioneer of sorts."

"I'll leave you to your research."

"Thanks." Nhyira takes another bite of the dessert.

This is delicious.

At 10PM Mrs. Denoble signals to Nhyira, "Library's closing hun."

"Can I have a few more minutes to take some pictures?"

"I'll go lock up in the back. Don't take long."

"I won't. I have another question."

"Yes?"

"Has anyone tampered with these books in the past?"

"Those books?" Mrs. Denoble laughs. "I doubt anyone cares about log books from the 50s."

"You sure?" Nhyira asks.

"Everything's digital these days. Most people don't go in the archives; they only care about the computers. Do you want me to ask the other staff members, in case they know something?"

"No thanks."

Although she knew it was time to go, Nhyira couldn't help but read a little more.

She was nearing the final page of one of the 1958 log books, when her eyes zeroed in on his name.

Gasping, she puts her hand to her mouth. There it was plain as day, the killer's name on more than one occasion; a frequent yet popular visitor to *Njapa*. No one would have suspected a thing. How could they?

*You little liar. It was **you** the whole time. You played me real good, but now...*

CHAPTER 51

Nhyira didn't care for sleep that night. She had a case to solve and refused to close her eyes.

The truth always comes out, no matter how long it takes. A phrase she'd often heard her parents say.

This truth took 4 decades to come to light, but it was time. The wrong person was behind bars and Nhyira was determined to make things right.

Her aunt had suffered many nights in that rotten prison and it was time for her release.

Rubbing the sleep from her eyes, Nhyira makes a final notation in her notebook. What started off as a mystery of letters, turned into solving a crime so eerie that no one in the country wanted to discuss it. The events of that day were sealed behind the smiles and frowns of the citizens.

Gathering her notebook and photo evidence, Nhyira dials the number for the DA's office.

She finally had the answer of who the real killer was.

But there was only one question on her mind…

Would anyone believe a 22-year-old foreigner?

187 Murder In Zaire Valley

CHAPTER 52

Not only was getting an appointment to see the DA daunting, but so was trying to convince him to reopen a case sealed shut with dust all over it.

Months had passed since Nhyira handed the DA her evidence and asked that he investigate the case further. The moment she walked into the courthouse, she knew the workers stared in disdain. Clearly word had gotten around of her inquisitiveness.

Everyone felt that she was out of order to undermine the older Celgagoan jurisdiction. But, facts were facts and they couldn't ignore it; especially when she threatened to take the story to the press.

The town had endured enough scandal and they wanted to investigate quietly.

Picking up the newspaper, Nhyira smiles as she reads the article.

40 Years of Lies, Corrected

November 1, 1998

Residents of *Njapa* received the shock of their lives when news broke out that 61 year old Poet Veisiejai was falsely accused and arrested in the death of her husband as stated in a 1958 article.

After two months of intense investigation, the DA has released a public statement and apology to Mrs. Poet Veisiejai.

"The mistakes of our forefathers would not continue. The entire country of Celgagoas humbly apologizes to you, Mrs. Veisiejai. Although apologies cannot make up for the past, we hope that amends can be made so that further citizens wouldn't be wrongfully accused and jailed."

The evidence - brought in by a recent addition to *Njapa*, 22-year-old Nhyira Enosis - was enough to convict 65 year old Rémire Embleton, a Construction Magnate living in *Minoda, Sopr. Vias* dubbed **The Boss**. Mr. Embleton – a former *Njapa* resident - was Mr. Veisiejai's business partner and Chief architect. The judge overseeing the case has sentenced him to two life sentences in the deepest part of **Kanomatton Underwater Prison**.

Mr. Embleton's wife has declined to comment.

Let this be a lesson to all, that no matter how long it takes, **justice will be served**.

In the meantime, we're eternally grateful to Ms. Enosis for reminding us to never give up on our families.

A live interview is scheduled with Mrs. Poet Veisiejai on Monday following her release.

Nhyira's phone rang off the hook, following the release of the newspaper article. She hadn't remembered giving any of the callers her phone number, but had every intention of going MIA for a few weeks until the popularity died down. Her uncle may have been **Mr. Popular**, but she had no desire to become <u>Ms. Popular</u>. Being **The Unscrambler** was enough status.

The day that Mr. Embleton was brought in for questioning Nhyira was right there front and center. The words he used against her could never be written in a book, but it didn't matter to Nhyira. Her aunt was now a free woman.

Sadly, Mr. Embleton had no remorse for his actions. He confessed that he stalked Mr. Veisiejai on several occasions begging him to split the blueprints so that he could make a name for himself in his new country to impress his future father-in-law. The day of Mr. Veisiejai's murder, he tried to get into the secret room, but was locked out. Kavos had changed the entry point.

Angrily, Mr. Embleton stormed out of the library noting the opulent window near the front entrance. An argument ensued and Kavos ran up the stairs. Rémire ran after Kavos and they tumbled down the stairs (hence his limp). In a bout of rage he picked up a saw left by workers and struck Mr. Veisiejai five times on the back of his head. When he noticed that Kavos was dead, he fled the scene of the crime and left the country through a stolen boat.

CHAPTER 53

The cameras flashed perpetually in front of Poet's face. A vast contrast from the day she was arrested. She didn't know how her niece was able to pull it off, but she was happy that the young woman insisted on speaking with her that first day.

Inhaling the fresh air, she begins to cry. At 61 years old she was free to start her life over. A stranger, turned family member, cared enough to hear her story and fight for her freedom.

"Mrs. Veisiejai, Mrs. Veisiejai. How does it feel to be a **Free Woman**? What is the first thing that you want to do?" a cameraman asks.

"There aren't words to describe how I feel," Poet explains. "I need a hot shower and a warm bed. That's all I want right now."

The paparazzo explodes in laughter.

"And is this your niece; the famous Nhyira Enosis?"

"Yes it is. Say something baby girl," Poet encourages.

Nhyira squints at the flashing lights. "I'm just happy that I was able to help. Justice was served. We're going to celebrate at **Mayleigh's Diner**. You're all welcome to join us."

The questions started pouring in as the duo head to the limo. Thankfully, the officers from the prison were able to keep the mob at bay.

Poet hugs Nhyira when the limo pulls off. "You did it."

"No, **we** did it. Without your help I wouldn't have been able to put the pieces together."

"Oh, don't underestimate what you did. You're a remarkable young lady you know that? I guess it runs in the family."

The women pause at the mention of the word **family**.

"Are you ready to go home?" Nhyira asks.

"That's your house sweetie, I'll find my way."

"Are you kidding me? My uncle built a massive house, it's **our** house."

"You're young. Enjoy it, I'll be fine," Poet declines.

"I won't take no for an answer."

"You are persistent. You're definitely Kavos' niece."

"What did the lawyer say?" Nhyira inquires.

"The bank's giving me my husband's frozen assets, worth a fortune now."

"That's amazing aunty."

"Yeah, what am I going to do with $80Million?"

"E-eighty? WOW!"

"He says it'll take a few days to write up everything, but he'll contact me with the details."

"I'm really happy for you."

"I'm going to give you half, Nhyira."

Nhyira shakes her head. "No, I can't accept that. I didn't do this for money."

"That's why I'm giving it to you; 1 million for every year of my life behind bars. You deserve more than money for giving me my freedom."

"I-I don't know what to say. Thanks aunty. What will you do with the rest?"

"I'll keep some and donate the majority of it to the **Royal Orphanage** in Voque. That money will help so many children. I don't need all that money. I have my freedom and my family. What more can a woman ask for?"

"I'll add to your donation."

"Have you ever considered becoming an **Investigative Journalist**?"

"No."

"You should. You have a real knack for solving crimes. The world isn't ready for your gift."

Nhyira hugs her aunt. "We're here. Welcome home aunty Poet."

Ms. Higüey crosses the street to the **Veisiejai House**. "I see that you're out," she mumbles to Poet.

"Lively, how have you been?"

"Don't try to be nice to me. I'm happy they found your husband's killer, but still mad at you for taking my man."

"I didn't want him then and I don't want him now," Poet grins.

"HMPH!" Lively replies.

Nhyira and Poet laughs.

"What are you laughing at child?"

"Nothing," Nhyira quips.

Lively rolls her eyes. "Now there'll be two foreigners living across from me? GREAT!" She turns and heads back to her house.

Nhyira and her aunt laugh even louder.

"Has she always been this nice to you?"

Nhyira nods. They walk inside the house. "I made your favorite."

Poet smiles at her niece. "*Pinkmoon Fries*?"

"Mmmhmmm."

"Bring it on girl. Bring. It. On."

"There's someone else that we both need to thank."

"Who?"

"It's a surprise."

Nhyira shivers in the cold as she waited for Mr. Colafranceschi to open his door. Zipping up her hoodie she knocks again.

"Who lives here?" her aunt asks.

"Wait for it."

The door opens. "Good night, Nhyira—" Mr. Colafranceschi pauses, "Are my eyes deceiving me?"

"What is it?" Nhyira inquires.

He looks at Poet. "Your face seems familiar," he states. "A little older, but is it possible... Poet?"

Poet begins to cry, "You remember me?"

"Come in, come in. It's chilly out. Have a seat. Drinks?"

"No thank you," the women say in unison.

"You always refuse my drinks Nhyira. To what do I owe this visit?"

"We're here on official **thank you** duty."

"Thank you?"

"If it wasn't for you and your records, none of this would be possible."

"I highly doubt that. You're a determined woman, Nhyira."

Poet takes the old man's hand. "Thank you sir, I am grateful. Thank you for being kind to me even when others treated me badly. You didn't make me feel like an outcast the day I entered this country."

"You'll always be that innocent girl I met all those years ago. I am happy that you're out. I should've done more."

"What you did to help Nhyira far outweighs anything else," Poet wipes tears from her eyes.

He smiles at her.

A thought plagues Nhyira's mind and she turns to the old man, "Mr. C, why did you say you liked my name?"

"You're an **Enosis**, I thought you knew. Your grandfather and I were best buds back in the day. We all grew up in *Grape Fjord* until I moved here in the 40s. Kedro Enosis was a character; strict at best, but cool. I met my wife in 1957 at the Governor's Ball in *Kanomatton. We* instantly fell in love. I left the Harbormaster job behind and sailed away with her that very day. I only returned 20 years ago when she died. It was the best decades of my life with that woman. Been living in isolation ever since. No point in enjoying life without her." He sighs, thinking about his wife.

"Well Mr. C, time for a change. Today your longtime friend was released from prison and we're going to celebrate. No more hiding," Nhyira announces.

Reggio looks at Poet. "She's serious?"

Poet grins, "'Fraid so."

CHAPTER 54

The door of **Mayleigh's Diner** pings, signifying the entrance of customers. The faces that entered were both familiar and new. Mayleigh immediately goes to take the trio's order.

"Mayleigh, this is my aunt, Mrs. Poet Veisiejai," Nhyira introduces.

"Nice to finally meet you ma'am," Mayleigh extends her hand.

"Thank you," Poet smiles and shakes Mayleigh's hand. "My niece has told me so much about you and your fabulous cooking."

"She's a charmer," Mayleigh nods.

"This is Mr. Reggio Colafranceschi," Nhyira introduces.

"Pleased to meet you sir," Mayleigh smiles. "I've heard a lot about your services for our town. I appreciate it."

"You're welcome dear," he replies. "What smells so good?"

"Can I answer?" Nhyira asks excitedly.

"Go right ahead. Tells us what your nose smells," Mayleigh beams.

"That Mr. C is Mayleigh's famous *Plumberry Pancakes*. They're going to be famous in Starr Islands one day. Mark my words."

"In that case, I'll have a half dozen. I'm paying for everyone's meal. Order whatever you want."

Nhyira looks at him. "Sir, we're here to thank you."

"A gentleman always pays. That's how I grew up. Have a seat ladies. I'll be right back."

"Where's he going?" Poet whispers.

"Looks like the jukebox," Nhyira notes.

Moments later, Nhyira squeals in excitement at the beginning chords of her favorite song.

"Do you know that song?" Reggio inquires.

"Do I? Of courseeeee. It's my favorite song. PRETTY MEMORIESSSS by *The Miseno Brothers*."

"You know good music," he counters. "Here's a fun fact. The *Miseno Brothers* are my wife's cousins."

"Get outta town," Nhyira gasps.

"I'm serious. That song was written for our wedding," Reggio reveals.

"Oh my gosh. History is AWESOME. You have to introduce me someday."

"Sure, whenever you're ready. They visit me all the time."

Nhyira's eyes lighten. "The *MISENO BROTHERS HAVE BEEN IN NJAPA AND I DIDN'T KNOW?*"

"They're older now. They keep a low profile. Who knew they still had admirers?"

"That would make my entire year. Can you arrange a meeting; a private concert? This day couldn't get any better," Nhyira claps.

"Is that so?" Akio approaches their table. "What are you squealing about, Ms. Enosis?"

Nhyira instantly blushes.

Poet looks at Akio. "Are you going to introduce me to your friend?"

"Excuse my manners. Akio, I'd like you to officially meet my aunt, Poet Veisiejai."

"Pleased to make your acquaintance ma'am," Akio kisses her hand.

"Likewise Warden. I'm glad to meet you on the **outside**."

Akio lets out a gentle laugh.

Nhyira continues, "And you remember Mr. Colafranceschi."

"Ah, the boyfriend," he grins shaking Akio's hand.

"He's not my—"

Akio puts a finger to her lips.

"Akio, what's going on?" Nhyira asks.

Taking her hands, Akio gets down on one knee.

"Uh, what are you doing?" Nhyira looks at him nervously.

Akio hushes her. "You're ruining a good moment Ms. Enosis."

"Stand up. I'm not going to marry you," Nhyira declines.

"You will one day, but for now… Nhyira, will you go on an official first date with me?"

"Huh?"

"Say yes," Reggio, Poet and Mayleigh sing.

Akio bats his eyes playfully at Nhyira. "Are you going to have me on my knees for long?"

"Okay Akio. I will go on an official date with you."

The trio in the background claps in excitement.

"Where are we going?"

"I know just the place…" Akio winks.

As they exited the diner, a thought crossed Nhyira's mind.

I think I'll enjoy life here in Njapa. I mean, what else could go wrong?

201 Murder In Zaire Valley

A Word From Theastarr

Thank you for reading MURDER IN ZAIRE VALLEY, Book 1 of the **Nhyira Files Mystery Series**. I hope you enjoyed it.

Nhyira's journey continues in Book 2, A FATAL BITE.

COMING IN 2021!!

Follow **Empress Royále Publishing** on Facebook and Instagram for information about upcoming books from Theastarr Valerie.

www.ingramcontent.com/pod-product-compliance
Lightning Source LLC
Chambersburg PA
CBHW032002240626
47153CB00003B/1092